MRS PARGETER'S PAST

Also by Simon Brett

The Decluttering Mysteries
THE CLUTTER CORPSE *
AN UNTIDY DEATH *
WASTE OF A LIFE *
A MESSY MURDER *

The Fethering Mysteries
BONES UNDER THE BEACH HUT
GUNS IN THE GALLERY *
THE CORPSE ON THE COURT *
THE STRANGLING ON THE STAGE *
THE TOMB IN TURKEY *
THE KILLING IN THE CAFÉ *
THE LIAR IN THE LIBRARY *
THE KILLER IN THE CHOIR *
GUILT AT THE GARAGE *
DEATH AND THE DECORATOR *
DEATH IN THE DRESSING ROOM *

The Mrs Pargeter Mysteries
MRS PARGETER'S PACKAGE
MRS PARGETER'S POUND OF FLESH
MRS PARGETER'S PLOT
MRS PARGETER'S POINT OF HONOUR
MRS PARGETER'S PRINCIPLE *
MRS PARGETER'S PUBLIC RELATIONS *
MRS PARGETER'S PATIO *

The Charles Paris Series
A RECONSTRUCTED CORPSE
SICKEN AND SO DIE
DEAD ROOM FARCE
A DECENT INTERVAL *
THE CINDERELLA KILLER *
A DEADLY HABIT *

The Major Bricket Mysteries
MAJOR BRICKET AND THE CIRCUS CORPSE

* *available from Severn House*

MRS PARGETER'S PAST

Simon Brett

SEVERN HOUSE

First world edition published in Great Britain and the USA in 2025
by Severn House, an imprint of Canongate Books Ltd,
14 High Street, Edinburgh EH1 1TE.

severnhouse.com

Copyright © Simon Brett, 2025

Cover and jacket design by Piers Tilbury

All rights reserved including the right of reproduction in whole or in part in any form. The right of Simon Brett to be identified as the author of this work has been asserted in accordance with the Copyright, Designs & Patents Act 1988.

British Library Cataloguing-in-Publication Data
A CIP catalogue record for this title is available from the British Library.

ISBN-13: 978-1-4483-1467-6 (cased)
ISBN-13: 978-1-4483-1865-0 (paper)
ISBN-13: 978-1-4483-1468-3 (e-book)

This is a work of fiction. Names, characters, places and incidents are either the product of the author's imagination or are used fictitiously. Except where actual historical events and characters are being described for the storyline of this novel, all situations in this publication are fictitious and any resemblance to actual persons, living or dead, business establishments, events or locales is purely coincidental.

No part of this book may be used or reproduced in any manner for the purpose of training artificial intelligence technologies or systems. This work is reserved from text and data mining (Article 4(3) Directive (EU) 2019/790).

All Severn House titles are printed on acid-free paper.

Typeset by Palimpsest Book Production Ltd., Falkirk, Stirlingshire, Scotland.
Printed and bound in Great Britain by TJ Books, Padstow, Cornwall.

The manufacturer's authorised representative in the EU for product safety is Authorised Rep Compliance Ltd, 71 Lower Baggot Street, Dublin D02 P593 Ireland (arccompliance.com).

Praise for the Mrs Pargeter Mysteries

'Fans will appreciate Brett's customary
inventiveness . . . and the wit'
Kirkus Reviews on *Mrs Pargeter's Patio*

'Mystery fans seeking pure escapist fun will be rewarded'
Publishers Weekly on *Mrs Pargeter's Public Relations*

'An enjoyable cozy'
Booklist on *Mrs Pargeter's Public Relations*

'Brett's customary wit and good humor abound'
Publishers Weekly Starred Review of
Mrs Pargeter's Principle

'Great fun, a delightfully madcap romp'
Booklist Starred Review of *Mrs Pargeter's Principle*

'The coziest of cozy reads'
Library Journal on *Mrs Pargeter's Principle*

About the author

Simon Brett worked as a producer in radio and television before taking up writing full-time. He is the author of more than a hundred books, including the much-loved Fethering Mysteries, the Charles Paris Mysteries and the Decluttering Mysteries, as well as the Mrs Pargeter Mysteries. In 2014, he was awarded the Crime Writers' Association's prestigious Diamond Dagger for sustained excellence and contribution to crime writing, and in the 2016 New Year's Honours he was awarded an OBE 'for services to literature'.

Married with three grown-up children, six grandchildren and a ginger cat called Douglas, he lives in an Agatha Christie-style village on the South Downs.

www.simonbrett.com

To Isla,
a dedication of her own,
with love

ONE

Everyone has a past and most people's pasts contain a lot of baggage. Mrs Pargeter was different. She had so carefully managed her past that its baggage could fit into one small, neat handbag. And the most important of that handbag's contents was the little black book bequeathed to her by the late Mr Pargeter.

She did not actively discourage people from asking about her past, but her close associates knew better than to be too curious. The important details that they knew about Mrs Pargeter were that she had had a blissfully happy marriage and that her husband was not a man to bring his work home with him. When asked by inquisitive types, like, say, the police, what the late Mr Pargeter had done for a living, she could, in all honesty, say that she didn't know.

The other essential bequest he had left to his wife was money. Oodles of the stuff. And he had bought a perfect building plot in Chigwell, Essex, on which the couple's dream house was to be erected. Sadly, the late Mr Pargeter had not survived to see the project finished, but his widow lived in some style in the completed mansion.

And when life in Essex became too dull, Mrs Pargeter could always nip up to London for a little pampering at Greene's Hotel, where the manager, 'Hedgeclipper' Clinton, would unfailingly have a suite available for her. It was, he frequently said, the least he could offer, given how much her late husband had done for him in his previous career.

So, how did Mrs Pargeter spend the oodles of cash that she had inherited? Apart from some essential pampering of herself, she channelled the funds into the kind of philanthropic causes of which the late Mr Pargeter would have approved. In many cases, these would involve helping out former associates of his who had fallen on hard times.

And it was on just such a mission of mercy that Mrs Pargeter found herself, having coffee in a private room at Greene's Hotel, being introduced to another of her husband's former associates. The man had worked in an accountancy capacity for the late Mr Pargeter, but he was called 'Short Head' Shimmings, because of his sideline as an unofficial bookmaker, and 'a short head' was the distance which most of the horses he backed lost by.

Also present at the meeting were two other gentlemen who had benefitted from the late Mr Pargeter's largesse. The aforementioned Hedgeclipper Clinton's route from running a café of dubious reputation to becoming the Greene's Hotel's manager had been eased by a considerable injection of cash from his former employer. And Truffler Mason, a tall, lugubrious figure with remarkable intuitive skills in rooting out evidence and finding missing persons, had been established by Mr Pargeter as a private investigator in the Mason de Vere Detective Agency. He was up for any kind of enquiry but would put everything else to one side if the summons came for him to help Mrs Pargeter.

Short Head Shimmings, it should be said, was built on the model of a pencil, uniformly thin, without visible protuberances other than his arms. He was taller than Truffler ... which was saying something. And the length of his face and neck gave the lie to his nickname of Short Head.

The hotelier and the private investigator had provided Mrs Pargeter with some useful background information about the case under discussion. As was his philanthropic habit, the late Mr Pargeter had set up Short Head Shimmings in his own betting shop at an ideal high street location in one of London's more salubrious eastern suburbs. And nothing should have got in the way of the business's booming success.

The thing that did get in the way of it, however, was that tragic quality which has been much written about by Shakespeare and various Greek playwrights, a 'fatal' flaw in Short Head Shimmings's personality. He was addicted to gambling.

As well as enjoying a wager, Short Head Shimmings was something of a dandy. Well, he would have been something of a dandy in the 1950s. Long jacket, drainpipe trousers and thick-soled shoes in true Teddy Boy style. And he wore his dyed black hair in an Elvis quiff. So, he was not afraid of making himself conspicuous.

This was something which might cause problems, given the difficulty in which the bookmaker found himself, as explained by Truffler Mason. 'Short Head was telling Hedgeclipper and me that he's got into a bit of trouble with debt.'

'"Debt"?' Mrs Pargeter echoed. Her hand reached instinctively to her handbag, in which she kept an item probably unfamiliar to the younger generation – a cheque book. She preferred the traditional ways of banking to all that vulnerable online business. 'If it's just a matter of money . . .'

'No,' said Truffler. 'Well, that is to say . . . obviously there is money involved . . . but the problem is more a matter of who the money is owed *to*.'

'Oh?' Mrs Pargeter sounded, as ever, blissfully innocent.

'The fact is,' Truffler went on, 'that, when Short Head began to have debt problems, he could not turn for help to traditional banking resources.'

'Why not?' came the ingenuous enquiry.

Truffler looked to Hedgeclipper Clinton for the best way to phrase the answer. 'Mr Shimmings's credit rating,' said the hotel manager smoothly, 'was, for some reason, not sufficiently robust for the banks to wish to do business with him.'

Mrs Pargeter nodded. She got the point.

'So, as a result . . .' said Truffler, 'Short Head turned to . . . less conventional sources of debt relief.'

'How'dja mean?' asked Mrs Pargeter.

Truffler turned to the bookie. 'I think it'd be simpler, Short Head, if you was to take over from here.'

'Very well,' came the tight-lipped response. The man spoke fastidiously, like some local council operative on the phone, being elaborately careful that his statements could not be misunderstood. 'The fact is, Mrs Pargeter, the more desperate one is for money, the more destructive are the terms on which one is able to borrow some. And, it has to be said, the less principled are the people who are prepared to lend it to you.

'Through acquaintances I had developed in the course of my

work as a bookmaker, I knew where some of my clients turned for financial assistance when the wretched horses consistently failed to oblige. According to the level of need in the punter, there was a graduated list of potential lenders. At the lowest level, there were almost-legal operators who charged very little more in interest than a legitimate bank would. But the higher you got up the hierarchy, the greater the risks. And, only when all other avenues had been explored and no other solution was possible, would anyone borrow money from the Batinga Brothers.'

The name prompted involuntary indrawn breaths from Truffler and Hedgeclipper.

'Mrs P, do you know who Short Head's talking about?' the hotelier asked, with some trepidation.

Mrs Pargeter looked at him with innocent curiosity. She was not surprised that he and Truffler recognised the reference, but they moved in very different circles from the ones she frequented. But the idea that she might have ever encountered such people as loan sharks . . . well, it was unthinkable.

'No,' she replied.

'Oh, that's strange. I thought you might remember how you got—'

'I don't think we need to go back into all that,' said Truffler forcefully. And he gave Hedgeclipper a stare which indicated he'd strayed onto dangerous ground. The hotelier looked suitably chastened.

'Anyway,' Short Head Shimmings went on, 'I'm afraid, I, rather incautiously, ended up borrowing money from the Batinga Brothers.'

The breath indrawn by Truffler and Hedgeclipper on the second iteration of the name was even deeper.

'And, to sum up,' Short Head concluded, 'I now owe the Batinga Brothers half a million and they want it back.'

'Well, I suppose that's reasonable,' Mrs Pargeter suggested tentatively. 'It is, after all, their money.'

'That is fair,' Truffler agreed lugubriously. 'What is not fair, though, is the means by which the Batinga Brothers encourage clients to stump up with the overdue payments on their debts.'

'Even less fair,' said Hedgeclipper, 'are methods which they use to punish clients who they don't think are ever going to pay their debts.'

'And which stage have you got to, Short Head?' asked Mrs Pargeter gently. 'Are the Batinga Brothers still encouraging you to stump up or . . .?'

The man's face blenched, as he said, 'No, I'm afraid they've moved on to the next stage. They've written off the chance of seeing their money back.'

'Don't worry,' said Mrs Pargeter calmly. 'We can pay it.'

Short Head Shimmings twisted his lips into disagreement. 'I'm afraid that won't be good enough.'

'You mean you had a deadline?' said Truffler Mason, who clearly knew how these things worked.

'Yes,' said the bookie. 'Midnight last Saturday.'

Truffler and Hedgeclipper exchanged quick grim looks, before the latter said, 'Well, congratulations on keeping out of their way for so long.'

A painful grimace from Short Head. 'Yes, but they're going to get me. They always do get people eventually.'

'That is their record,' said Truffler. 'Very definitely.'

'But surely,' Mrs Pargeter interposed, 'if they get paid the money now . . .?'

A slow shake of the head from the private investigator. 'So you might think, but no. It's a matter of pride for them, see. The Batinga Brothers have a reputation to maintain, in their community. And I don't mean their reputation as respectable businessmen in the City. I mean their reputation in . . . less salubrious areas of life. Everyone will know that they've given Short Head a deadline. It's like a kind of contract.'

'In more ways than one,' Hedgeclipper commented dourly.

'No amount of payment could save Short Head's bacon now,' said Truffler. 'Twice as much as what's owing, ten times as much . . . the Batinga Brothers wouldn't take it. They'd have lost face, you see. If it got . . . round . . . in their community . . . that debtors could buy themselves out of a Batinga Brothers deadline . . . well, people'd start to think they were a soft touch. And the Batinga Brothers wouldn't stand for that. It'd destroy the image they've spent many years – and many crimes – building up.'

'That's right.' Short Head Shimmings looked even gloomier. 'They're probably going to get me, anyway, Mrs Pargeter, but I heard from some mates that you'd helped out other former associates of your late husband and I thought . . . well, it's worth a try.'

'And you were absolutely right to think that,' said Mrs Pargeter. 'If there's any way I can continue Mr Pargeter's charitable work, then I feel it my duty to do my best. Don't worry, Short Head, we'll get this sorted.'

'I can't thank you enough.' The relief had brought the bookie almost to the edge of tears. 'When I think of all your late husband did for me, Mrs Pargeter, and how I've let him down, well, I—'

'Don't worry about that.' She was suddenly businesslike. 'So, Truffler, what is our plan of action? What do we need to do?'

'First thing, Mrs P,' he replied, 'is we need to find a safe house for Short Head. He's done very well to escape the Batinga Brothers' attentions since midnight on Saturday, but they'll track him down soon enough.'

'Very well,' said the widow. 'Then that's what we must do. Can I leave the details to you, Truffler?'

'Of course you can, Mrs P. I'll get on to the appropriate organisers and we'll stow him away somewhere where even the Mounties would never find him.'

'Good. So, what else do we need to do?'

Truffler, Hedgeclipper and Short Head Shimmings all exchanged awkward looks of gloom.

'The next thing we'd have to do, I guess,' said the hotel manager, 'if we're going to ensure Short Head's safety until he dies, is to completely dismantle the Batinga Brothers' criminal empire.'

There was a silence, before Mrs Pargeter said, 'Right. Then that's what we'd better do. We will completely dismantle the Batinga Brothers' criminal empire.'

Truffler Mason, whose default mood was gloom, sounded even gloomier as he intoned, 'I wouldn't bet on it, Mrs P.'

'Oh?' Short Head Shimmings couldn't resist the challenge. 'I would.'

TWO

Short Head Shimmings's security in the short term was easily arranged. It happened with some frequency that former colleagues of Hedgeclipper Clinton came to him in need of sanctuary. The reasons for that need varied, but in most cases the imperative was to keep out of sight of people who very much wanted to make contact with them. The pursuers could be debt collectors, bailiffs, gamblers who felt they'd been cheated at cards, spurned mistresses, husbands of spurned mistresses, angry wives and, quite frequently, hitmen.

With a view to providing this facility, when he took over Greene's Hotel (with finance generously supplied by the late Mr Pargeter), Hedgeclipper had one area of the building specially converted into what was known (to the very few aware of its existence) as 'the Safe Suite'. Though the interior décor matched that of all the hotel's other luxury accommodation, behind the surface adornments were walls of steel. Inside the double doors with their highly polished brass fittings was a steel shutter which, at the touch of a button, could descend to isolate the guest inside.

The basic building work on the conversion had been done by another of the late Mr Pargeter's former associates, a builder called Concrete Jacket. He was expert at his craft and had also masterminded the construction of 'Lionel's Den', Mrs Pargeter's substantial mansion in Chigwell.

The only drawback of employing Concrete as a builder was his tendency to be absent from the jobs he was working on for considerable stretches of time. And 'stretch' was the operative word, because during those absences he was accommodated in one or other HMP prisons. If anyone asked him about this regrettable habit, he would tell them it was not down to criminality, just bad luck. He had an unfortunate propensity for working with associates who regularly shafted him and framed him for crimes he hadn't committed. At least, that was Concrete Jacket's own story – and the one he resolutely stuck to.

Once the building work was complete, the protective qualities of the Greene's Hotel Safe Suite had been sternly tested before interior decoration took place. The shutter proved impervious to penetration by any bullets, though anti-tank weapons did make small dents. Nor was it breached by the detonation of a hand grenade rolled up against it (though, after that test, the hotel landing did require a bit of refurbishment).

The suite featured an iron-clad lift down to a specially protected area of the hotel's underground car park. If the temporary resident needed transport away from the place, a suitably armoured vehicle could be waiting for them in a space shut off by a metal shutter of the same security spec as the one upstairs.

One of the suite's other amenities was a bombproof dumb waiter, by means of which the incarcerated guest could enjoy the gastronomic delights of the Greene's Hotel kitchen and the pick of its wine cellar.

It should be pointed out that the Safe Suite had, on occasion, been used in a custodial rather than protective capacity. It sometimes happened that people, who had offended against the strict moral code of the late Mr Pargeter and his associates, needed to be kept secure for a few days. 'In remand', as it were, until the precise nature of their punishment had been decided.

Basically, then, the Batinga Brothers had no chance of getting at Short Head Shimmings, so long as he was in Greene's Hotel's Safe Suite.

Because of the way it would restrict his life, however, keeping him there for more than a few days would be impractical. A more permanent arrangement would have to be made.

Fortunately, Mrs Pargeter and Truffler Mason knew the perfect person to make such an arrangement.

* * *

In the taxi on the way there, Truffler mentioned a minor problem that might arise when hiding their bookmaker. 'Short Head Shimmings has a mother,' he announced.

'So does everyone,' said Mrs Pargeter equably.

'Yes, but his is one of the, er . . . clinging type.'

'You mean he's never got married?'

'Exactly. He's one of those sad cases where the apron strings have taken on the qualities of a straitjacket.'

'Ah. I'm with you.'

'So, he's refusing to be hidden anywhere too far away from her.'

'And where does she live?'

'Southend.'

'Which is where Short Head also lives. With her, presumably?'

'Yes, Mrs P. They have lived in the same house ever since his father, the late Mr Shimmings, died. And his mother insists on seeing her Cecil every day.'

'Cecil?'

'Yes. That's his real name.'

'Poor soul.'

'Runs in the family. His mother's called Athena.'

'Oh dear.'

Mrs Pargeter tried to piece things together. 'So, what he's asking for . . . or, maybe, what his mother's asking for . . .?'

'It's the latter.'

'Let me get this straight. She's demanding that her son – Cecil – is to be hidden somewhere where he'll be out of reach of the notoriously vengeful Batinga Brothers, but at the same time for him to be near enough his home in Southend to see his dear old mum every day?'

'That's exactly it, Mrs P.'

'Well, there's no way he can be in Southend, is there? That's the first place the Batingas are going to look. No, his dear old mum is clearly not going to get her way on this one, is she, Truffler?'

'I'd like to think you were right, but Mrs Shimmings is a very strong woman.'

The 'Huh' with which Mrs Pargeter greeted this was distinctive. It made absolutely clear that she had dealt with strong women before and was quite happy – even relished the idea – that she would be called on to deal with another.

Hamish Ramon Henriquez did no publicity for his services, but word of mouth kept him quite busy enough. (That word, though, was only circulated amongst a specific selection of mouths.) The discreet nature of his travel agency was exemplified by the small brass plate reading 'HRH Travel' by the door of the impressive Berkeley Square three-storied townhouse which contained his office.

Some form of CCTV must have alerted the staff inside, because the door opened before Truffler's long finger had reached the bell push. He and Mrs Pargeter were greeted by a smiling, immaculately groomed girl in a charcoal-grey uniform. On one side of her jacket was woven in gold thread a discreet 'HRH' logo. On the other, an equally discreet gold badge identified her as 'Lauren'.

'Welcome, Mrs Pargeter and Mr Mason,' she said with beautifully enunciated vowels. 'HRH is so looking forward to seeing you.'

By now, she was at the Reception desk. She pressed a button and another smiling, immaculately groomed girl in a charcoal-grey uniform appeared. 'Megan will take you upstairs to HRH's office,' said Lauren.

'If you'd like to come this way . . .' Megan's vowels were just as beautifully enunciated as Lauren's. She ushered them to the lift, whose doors opened immediately. On the second floor, she led them through a long office, on either side of which more smiling, immaculately groomed girls in charcoal-grey uniforms were either working on laptops or talking on mobile phones with, it goes without saying, beautifully enunciated vowels. Passing through, Mrs Pargeter and Truffler Mason heard snatches of their chatter.

'. . . at the airport, make sure your taxi driver is wearing a red bandana with white polka dots. He will take you to the beach house in Malibu where your target is staying. There is only one bodyguard who always takes a nap after lunch . . .'

'. . . and when you arrive at your room in the hotel, you'll find there's a semi-automatic pistol hidden in the cistern of the toilet . . .'

'. . . once you're in Bogota, take a taxi to Bolivar Square and get out there. To the north, behind the Palace of Justice you will find a small backstreet called Calle Camilo Torres Tenorio. In a tailor's shop called Gonzago, your disguises will be ready for you . . .'

'. . . I can assure you that the tour guide in Manila will supply you with body armour . . .'

Truffler Mason cast a slightly anxious eye towards Mrs Pargeter, worrying what she might be making of what they were hearing.

'Goodness me,' she said innocently, 'I can't understand what they're on about.'

The door at the end of the room burst open to reveal the tall figure of Hamish Ramon Henriquez, his arms wide in greeting. 'Mrs Pargeter! It has been far too long since I have seen you! And, Truffler, what a pleasure!'

His voice, marinated in the kind of port that is laid down at birth in only the best of British aristocratic families, was at odds with his appearance. Though his vowels had been aged, along with his tweed suit, in the cellars of English stately homes, his look was that of a more robust Don Quixote. Mediterranean dark-brown skin, black eyes either side of a beakish nose, long white hair parted in the middle and a luxuriant white moustache above his sensuous lips.

Calling out an order for coffee to another smiling, immaculately groomed girl in a charcoal-grey uniform whose name badge read 'Deryn', he ushered them into his office. It was a space of dark polished panelling, finely bound books and leather furniture, of the kind frequently seen in television adaptations of Sherlock Holmes. Beside his massive desk was an angled antique globe on which his long fingers could instantly find the remotest part of the world.

'So, Mrs Pargeter,' he demanded once they were all seated, 'what can I do for you? Anything. As you know, anything. When I think how much your husband helped me when I was starting out in this business . . . Was it a holiday you were after?'

'No, HRH. It was more a matter of . . . accommodation.'

'For yourself?'

'No, for someone else.'

'Short Head Shimmings,' Truffler contributed. 'Don't know if you ever met him in the course of your work back in the day . . .?'

'I heard the name,' the travel agent replied, in a manner which suggested not all he'd heard about the name was good. 'Had a rather destructive gambling habit, I seem to recall. At least, he did back then.'

'I'm afraid he still has,' said Mrs Pargeter. 'And I'm afraid it's still getting him into trouble.'

'Oh dear. And where is he at this moment?'

'Secure in Greene's Hotel,' Truffler replied.

'In the Safe Suite?'

The private investigator nodded.

'But he can't stay there forever,' said Mrs Pargeter, 'so we were wondering whether you might have a suggestion of somewhere more permanent for him?'

'Of course.'

There was a moment's delay while Deryn brought in a Georgian silver coffee set on a Georgian silver tray and the drinks were poured into bone china cups (of course on bone china saucers).

Then HRH reached into a drawer of his desk and produced a glossy brochure. Its title read: 'Safe As Houses – HRH Travel has the widest range of Safe Houses in the world. The ultimate Getaways! We've found destinations where you'll never be found!'

He passed it across. 'I'm sure we'll have the right place for Short Head Shimmings. Our track record in this area is exceptional. The ways in which we hid Shergar and Lord Lucan are still talked about with awe in the crim—' Seeing the puzzlement in Mrs Pargeter's violet eyes, he amended the word he was about to articulate. 'In the relevant community.

'We have secluded hideaways all over the world. Patagonia,

the Amazon Rainforest, depths of the Congo, the Australian outback . . . you name it, we have suitable accommodation there. And there are various grades of security, rising up to twenty-four-hour surveillance with armed guards. The various packages are, needless to say, priced accordingly.'

'Money's not an object,' said Mrs Pargeter. She never said those words — and she said them quite often — without another little surge of gratitude for the generosity of her late husband.

'No, no!' The travel agent was fulsome in his apologies. 'I wasn't suggesting that you should pay, Mrs P.'

'I'm quite happy to.'

'But I would be deeply unhappy were you ever to pay for any of HRH's services. When I think what your late husband did for—'

Mrs Pargeter, who had heard this litany of praise a few times before, spoke over him, saying, 'That's very kind of you.'

The travel agent cleared his throat. 'Returning to Short Head Shimmings's little . . . er, difficulty, was there somewhere particular you had in mind, Mrs P?'

'There's no way it's going to be Southend,' she said, 'but I still think it's got to be in this country.'

Beneath the white moustache, the travel agent's lips turned downwards. 'Ah. Well, that does rather limit the options.'

'You mean you haven't got anywhere suitable?'

'Certainly not, Mrs P.' He was offended by the aspersion she had unwittingly cast on the efficiency of his organisation. 'It simply means that more risk assessment has to be undertaken. Obviously, the first place those wishing to retrieve monies owing from Short Head Shimmings . . .' He stopped to check. 'That is why he needs to make himself scarce, I presume?'

Lugubriously, Truffler Mason confirmed that to be the case.

'And presumably we're talking about gambling debts?'

'We are.'

'Well, the first place any debt collector would look for him would be the land of his birth. It's not a problem, Mrs P, just something that requires careful planning.'

'I'm sure you're very good at that, HRH.'

A beam spread across his olive-coloured face. 'I most

certainly am,' he said with satisfaction, 'which explains the unrivalled success of HRH Travel.'

'Good for you,' said Mrs Pargeter.

The beam grew broader. 'One thing I feel I should ask . . .'

'Yes?'

'Because it affects the level of security I will look for in my selection of suitable accommodation.'

'Of course.'

'So, who is it Short Head owes money to?'

'The Batinga Brothers,' said Truffler.

HRH let out a low whistle. 'And you're telling me he's still alive?'

'So far.'

'Maximum security then.' The travel agent looked troubled. 'The Batinga Brothers have a nasty reputation for always tracking down the people who've put their noses out of joint.'

'I know that,' said Truffler.

'Had Short Head thought of plastic surgery?' asked HRH. 'Might be an additional safeguard. Because, if he does want to go down that route, I've got a direct line to Melting Maurice.'

Mrs Pargeter told the travel agent that she'd met the gentleman in question. And knew that he derived his nickname from the old joke about the plastic surgeon who sat by the fire and melted. 'Delightful man,' she said. 'But I don't think we want to go down that route in this case. Not yet, anyway. Short Head Shimmings gave the impression of being rather proud of his looks.'

'Very well. If you say so, Mrs P.' HRH still looked dubious.

'But you do think you'll be able to find somewhere suitable for him?' asked Mrs Pargeter, a little anxiously.

Hamish Ramon Henriquez had recaptured all of his confidence as he replied, 'Of course I will, Mrs P.'

He pressed a button on the intercom system. 'Corinne,' he said. 'Code V.'

Within seconds, there was a knock on the door and, on being granted admission, another smiling, immaculately groomed girl in a charcoal-grey uniform appeared. Her lapel badge, unsurprisingly, read 'Corinne'.

She handed across a loose-leaf folder.

'The file you wanted, HRH.' More beautifully cut-glass vowels, of course.

'Corinne,' he said, 'is one of my most senior staff members. Entrusted with the really top-secret stuff.' He then introduced her to his guests.

'A pleasure to meet you,' said Mrs Pargeter.

'An honour for me,' said the girl. 'I've heard so much about you.'

Mrs Pargeter chuckled. 'All good, I hope.'

'Better than good.'

Mrs Pargeter beamed.

'Thank you, Corinne.' HRH dismissed her with a courteous nod. She smiled a perfect smile and exited the office.

HRH flicked through the file contents. On its front cover, Mrs Pargeter noticed, was a label reading 'NowhAirBnB'. His long fingers quickly found the page he wanted.

'I think this will be perfect for your requirements, Mrs P,' he announced.

THREE

Gary, the chauffeur, was another beneficiary of the late Mr Pargeter's wisdom in career planning for his associates. When they worked together, it was the young man's ability to drive away from places quickly which was called on most, and skidpan training was arranged to improve those skills. But his generous sponsor also arranged classes in management studies, which would stand him in good stead when he set up a private car hire business. And it was the late Mr Pargeter who had provided the finance for his protégé's first fleet of vehicles.

One of the qualities of the service Gary offered had always been its range. Cars were available for every occasion, from stretch limos to holiday hatchbacks. And there were a few 'special cars' which had been customised to meet highly individual requirements.

As the company expanded, Gary did less actual driving himself, but he would still instantly drop everything to make himself available if the call came from Mrs Pargeter. Though there was an age difference, and it was something he would never admit to anyone, Gary did hold something of a candle for his former boss's widow. There was about her an amplitude, both of spirit and of flesh, which he found indefinably, but strongly, alluring.

He was elated to hear her voice at the end of the phone that morning and instantly cleared his calendar of other commitments. The phone was then passed over to Truffler Mason, who spelled out the details of what was required for this particular job.

Instantly, Gary realised that he was going to need to use one of his 'special cars'.

The practice of customising cars goes right back to the birth of the automobile industry. At first, all vehicles were virtually bespoke creations. And, subsequently, when mass production took over, owners had always wanted little extras added which would distinguish their own proud possessions from the run-of-the-mill versions. In many cases, it used to be the bodywork that was personalised. For royalty and the upper echelons of society, the armorial bearings which had decorated the sides of their horse-drawn carriages soon started to appear on their horseless ones.

And many an early petrolhead had had their standard-issue engine replaced with something a lot more powerful.

Customising the boots of cars was less common, but Gary owned two in which that part of the vehicle had undergone detailed refinement. He thought of them, rather whimsically, as the 'In-Boot Car' and the 'Out-Boot Car'.

The former, the In-Boot Car, had been supplied with no new amenities. The only adjustments made to its spec were in the area of security. Not only was the boot's interior reinforced with steel, its locks were designed to resist the world's most skilled safe-breaker. So, in the event of – to take a random example – a person or persons armed with gelignite trying to release someone incarcerated inside the boot, their attempt would be doomed to failure. It goes without saying that the people destined to be locked in that boot were not Gary's friends . . . nor indeed friends of any of the late Mr Pargeter's associates.

Those who were favoured, however, got a much better deal in the Out-Boot Car. Though the space was equally secure, it boasted a much superior level of luxury. The bottom of the boot had been lowered, so that its passenger could sit in comfort. State-of-the-art lights, sound system and television were available, along with a fridge stocked with Greene's Hotel's best champagne and party nibbles.

Should the occupant wish to lie down, the seating system converted into a very comfortable bed. And should the occupant be lucky enough to have someone to share his accommodation, that bed easily converted into a double. The vehicle was used to convey friends of the late Mr Pargeter's associates out of tricky situations and into places of greater safety.

It goes without saying that the Out-Boot Car was the one used to take Short Head Shimmings from the Safe Suite at Greene's Hotel to his destination.

And it also goes without saying that it was waiting for him, with Gary in the driving seat, in the secure area of the Greene's Hotel car park the following morning.

Mrs Pargeter was always thorough in her philanthropy. If she committed herself to helping one of her late husband's former associates, then it was a point of honour with her to see the job through.

So, it was no surprise that, rather early the following morning, accompanied by Truffler Mason, she was sitting in the back seat of the Out-Boot Car as Gary drove it smoothly into the underground garage of Greene's Hotel. Hedgeclipper Clinton, who had been expecting them, stepped out through the door which led to Reception. Gary lowered his window and the hotelier greeted them. Mrs Pargeter could not help observing that he seemed extremely agitated.

'Don't worry, Hedgeclipper,' she said cheerily. 'We'll soon have Short Head Shimmings on his way and you can stop worrying about the Batinga Brothers destroying your lovely hotel.'

'That is not what I'm worried about, in fact, Mrs Pargeter.'

'Got a problem, have we?' asked Truffler mournfully.

'We have a bit, yes,' Hedgeclipper replied.

'Tell us the worst. They haven't got to Short Head somehow, have they?'

'No, no, he's fine. But the thing is . . .'

'What?' asked Mrs Pargeter urgently.

'Short Head's been all set to go for this since I told him about it last night . . .'

'But? There obviously is a "but".'

'Yes, Mrs P, there is. You may be aware that Short Head's very close to his mother.'

'Truffler told me that. They've always lived together.'

'Exactly. So . . . well, anyway . . . he asks me yesterday if his mum can come and visit him . . . you know, that evening, before he goes away. And I can't see any harm in that.'

'You should have checked with us,' said Truffler Mason accusingly.

'Yes, you should,' Gary agreed.

'I thought it'd be OK,' said Hedgeclipper, 'so I send a car to Southend and let her into the Safe Suite. And I organise a nice meal to be sent up to them from the kitchens.

'I've said I'll let her out at ten o'clock and a car'll take her back home. Which I think is all fine, so I go up at the appointed time and I open the Safe Suite. And, yes, they've finished their dinner and they say how much they've enjoyed it. Mrs Shimmings says it was really nice, and Short Head agrees. But when I ask her to leave, she won't budge.'

'Ah,' said Mrs Pargeter.

'She said that she's not going to allow Cecil – that's what she calls him, Cecil – to go anywhere without her. Particularly anywhere dangerous. So, I'm afraid, when you get into the secure part of this garage, there won't be just one person coming down in the lift from the Safe Suite. There'll be two.'

'Why on earth didn't you tell us there was a problem before now?' demanded Truffler.

'Yes, why didn't you?' demanded Gary.

'I kept thinking,' said the wretched Hedgeclipper, 'through the night, that I'd be able to make her change her mind. But I couldn't. She's a very strong woman,' he concluded feebly.

'Is she?' said Mrs Pargeter. 'We'll see about that.'

Short Head Shimmings's mother was, as they had been told, called Athena. For obvious reasons, Melita Pargeter had no prejudices against people with unusual first names. In fact, she had no prejudice against anyone (obviously, that didn't include politicians and estate agents).

Athena Shimmings was tiny, under five foot. To have produced the towering Short Head, genetic logic suggested that her late husband must have been some kind of giant. But, from the moment Mrs Pargeter met her, it was clear who was in charge in that particular mother/son relationship.

The Out-Boot Car was in the secure part of the Greene's Hotel car park when Short Head and Athena Shimmings emerged from the lift.

Hedgeclipper tried again to sort things out. 'No, Short

Head,' he said urgently. 'It's only going to be you. We can't take anyone else. The risk from the Batinga Brothers is just too great.'

'I was trying to tell Mum—'

But that was as far as he got. Mrs Pargeter reckoned that was about as far as he ever got in conversations with his mother.

'Don't listen to Cecil,' said Athena Shimmings. 'He doesn't know what he wants half the time. But he does know that, whenever he has to go away for more than one night, I go with him. That way, everything stays nice.'

'Perhaps,' Truffler tried to intercede. 'But, Mrs Shimmings, I'm not sure that you fully understand why Short – I mean Cecil – has to go away on this occasion.'

'Of course I do,' she said testily. 'He has to go away for work.'

'But do you know what his work is?'

'Do you take me for an idiot, whoever you are?'

'My name's Truff—'

But Athena Shimmings couldn't have been less interested in who he was. 'Cecil works as a bookkeeper.'

'Are you sure you don't mean a bookm . . .?' Truffler's words trickled away in response to the vigorous semaphore gestures Short Head was making behind his mother's back.

'I have always known what my son does professionally,' Athena continued serenely on her way. 'Cecil talks to me about his work. He's got a very nice job. And I fully understand the level of secrecy that is involved in some of the things he has to do. When he is doing the books for government departments, obviously there are criminals out there who would like to stop him doing his public duty. But Cecil is such a diligent and loyal worker that he is prepared to face the inherent risks that come with his position of trust.

'And it's unfortunate that a lot of the places where Cecil has done the books for them, like banks and building societies, often get robbed afterwards. When it does happen, Cecil always says it's a good thing that, at least, their books are in good order. Whatever the challenge, Cecil always does a nice job.'

Mrs Pargeter decided it was time she cut short this paean

of praise to the virtues of Short Head Shimmings. 'I appreciate everything you are saying, Mrs Shimmings, but I feel I should point out that the level of risk in this particular instance is exceptionally high.'

'I'm aware of that. Cecil always tells me the details of what he's doing. And I know that doing the books for the Batinga Brothers is a matter of great importance.'

Looks were exchanged between Truffler Mason, Hedgeclipper Clinton, Gary and Short Head Shimmings. The first three looked shocked by the lie that Athena Shimmings had swallowed. The fourth looked embarrassed and apologetic for telling it.

Mrs Pargeter took the initiative. 'Mrs Shimmings, I'm afraid you have to recognise the facts of the current situation. On this occasion, we are under pressure of time. We have a long journey ahead of us. And I'm afraid there is no possibility that you can travel with Cecil.'

Athena's response was not verbal. She turned round and faced her son. The top of her head was level with the middle button on his Teddy Boy drape jacket. She stared upwards.

The other four could not see the nature of the look she fixed on him. But it must have been one that, from childhood onward, had surgically removed his spine. He capitulated instantly.

'Sorry,' he said to his potential saviours. 'I can't go unless Mum comes too.'

And that was it. Further arguments were raised against the condition Short Head Shimmings was imposing, but to no avail. Rueful looks amongst the people in the garage who weren't called Shimmings showed acceptance of the inevitable. Either Short Head must be abandoned to the revenge of the Batinga Brothers, or they must accept his – or rather Athena Shimmings's – terms. Grudgingly, the deal was agreed.

Mrs Pargeter was more grudging than anyone. She didn't enjoy being beaten, least of all by an over-possessive mother who had totally emasculated her son.

Her mood was only partially improved by the turning-down of the suggestion that Athena Shimmings should travel on the back seat of the Out-Boot Car with Mrs Pargeter and Truffler.

The latter insisted that, because mother and son cohabited, she was probably as recognisable to the Batinga Brothers as Short Head was.

So, it was agreed that Athena should also be accommodated, along with her son, in the customised boot. (The designers who'd created amenities for two there had not been thinking of the space being shared by a female companion of the maternal kind.)

Mrs Pargeter's annoyance was not alleviated when Short Head Shimmings, before he joined his mother in the boot, whispered to her, 'Apologies for all that business about book-keeping, Mrs P. It's just my mum likes everything to be nice. And I'll never tell another lie as long as I live.'

'I wouldn't bet on it,' said an unbelieving Mrs Pargeter.

'I would, though,' was Short Head Shimmings's knee-jerk reaction. 'How much?'

'Short Head, we are not talking about gambling. We are talking about you lying to your mother about what you do. How did that come about?'

'Well, you know how it is, don't you?'

'No,' Mrs Pargeter replied magnificently, 'I do not know how it is.'

'What I mean is, sometimes we have to gloss over details of our past, stuff we've done that might have been a bit dodgy, don't we?'

Her look demanded further explanation. 'Like,' said Short Head, 'haven't you ever been in a situation, where you had to pretend that something dead iffy was actually legit?'

'I have no idea what you're talking about,' said Mrs Pargeter with glacial bewilderment.

Only Gary knew where they were going. In making the arrangements, HRH had followed a principle often quoted by the late Mr Pargeter. 'The fewer people know about something, the fewer people can reveal it, even under extreme forms of persuasion.'

So, HRH had only confided to Gary the NowhAirBnB address where Short Head Shimmings – now, unfortunately, with his mother along for the ride – would be safe from the attentions of the Batinga Brothers.

For a few moments, Mrs Pargeter continued to smart from her failure to defeat Athena Shimmings, but her naturally sanguine nature soon reasserted itself.

As she always found when she did the assessment, she had more reasons to be happy than sad. She was embarking on a new adventure, surrounded by the people who she liked and trusted more than anyone else in the world.

Not for the first time, she glowed with gratitude for the way the late Mr Pargeter continued to protect her from beyond the grave.

FOUR

The Out-Boot Car was not designed to act as a hearse, but on occasion it had been used for not dissimilar purposes. Certainly, one of its special features enabled the vehicle to be backed up to a door and to shield from view anybody – or any body – being transferred from boot to building. The fact that Gary had reversed up against a church porch made the comparison to a hearse even more apposite. And, in fact, that entrance to the church was known as 'the coffin door'.

But it wasn't a coffin that was transferred on this occasion. It was two people, Short Head Shimmings and his mother Athena.

Mrs Pargeter and Truffler waited till Gary had closed the special boot lid and parked the car more conventionally on the church drive. Then they followed him inside.

Mrs Pargeter didn't know what she was expecting, but it certainly wasn't being enwrapped in a warm hug. Or hearing a familiar booming voice from a vicar saying, 'My dear creature! What an enormous pleasure to see you!'

If you happen to be called 'The Reverend Smirke', there's only one nickname possible for you.

'Hello, "Holy",' said Mrs Pargeter, greeting someone she hadn't seen for a long time.

It goes without saying that 'Holy' Smirke had been an associate of the late Mr Pargeter. With characteristic generosity, the philanthropist had once again spotted potential and developed it. In the case of Holy Smirke, there had been a pointer in his appearance. He somehow looked like a vicar, all bumbling earnestness. And, though not ordained, he had frequently worn a dog collar for his work. Sadly, that work had not involved treading the path of righteousness. It had mostly involved conning little old ladies out of their life savings.

So, when Mrs Pargeter's husband looked to point the sinner in a new direction, it had made sense to create for him the reality of what he had for so long pretended to be. Mr Pargeter sponsored the young Smirke through theological college and saw to it that he got properly ordained.

Mrs Pargeter had not known Holy in his pre-ordination days, but their paths had crossed when he was Priest in Charge of St-Crispin-in-the-Closet, a tiny medieval church in the City of London. At that time, he was sharing his vicarage with a Frenchwoman called Ernestine, a brilliant cook whose cassoulet won plaudits from everyone who tasted it. Ernestine also had that uniquely French attitude that she would not think of allowing age in any way to diminish her glamour.

Mrs Pargeter's investigation on that occasion into the activities of a man called 'Hair-Trigger' Harrison had involved going deeply into the past of her late husband. It had also involved Holy Smirke getting kidnapped.

Her shock at re-meeting the vicar in such unlikely circumstances meant it took a moment for Mrs Pargeter to take in his new surroundings. The building they were in, she had noted when Gary drove the Out-Boot Car through the gates, was called 'The Parish Church of St Perpetua the Martyr'. The interior was small and simple; its origins quite possibly going back to Saxon times. The modest altar was looked down on by a carved Christ on the Cross. Marble plaques on the walls celebrated the lives of long-dead parishioners. The wooden pews looked as though they had been there as long as the uneven paving on which they stood. A large tomb at the back of the church was topped by the carved effigies of a medieval armoured knight and his lady. The knight's legs were crossed.

'You're the last person I expected to find here,' Mrs Pargeter went on.

'Well, I am a vicar,' Holy Smirke asserted, reasonably enough. 'Where else would you expect to find me but in a church?'

'But out of London, Holy? I somehow always think of you as an urban creature.'

'A leopard can change its spots,' he said with a sly wink.

'And I have proved capable of changing mine more than once, for reasons of expediency. Back when I was working with your husband—'

'I've no idea what you're talking about, Holy,' said Mrs Pargeter serenely. 'You remember Truffler and Gary?'

'Yes, good to see you, maties.'

Cheery greetings were exchanged.

'Incidentally, Holy,' said Mrs Pargeter looking round the church interior, 'only moments ago, two members of the Shimmings family came in here. And I can't help noticing, there's no sign of them.'

'Ah,' said Holy Smirke guilefully. 'Why do you think this particular service of HRH is called "NowhAirBnB"? One moment people are here, the next they have disappeared into thin air.'

'So, where've they gone?' asked Truffler.

'The very question,' said the vicar, 'which I am sure is currently much on the minds of the Batinga Brothers. But the chances of those villains actually locating their quarry are slender indeed.'

He moved towards the tomb at the back of the church. 'Here we see the memorial to Sir Geoffrey de Manville and his lady wife Isabella. His legs are crossed which, according to some authorities – largely discredited now – means that he went on a crusade.

'I, however, can demonstrate a considerably more useful function for the crossed leg.'

As he spoke, Holy Smirke took hold of the carved limb and lifted it. Silently, the whole tomb, with its unmoving effigies on top, lifted up at one end and moved from the horizontal to the perpendicular.

Revealed, in the space where the great stone rectangle had stood, was an opening, from the top of which a silent escalator led down to the unknown depths of the Parish Church of St Perpetua the Martyr.

'Let me lead the way,' said Holy Smirke. 'Mrs Pargeter, I think it's time you saw the amenities of our NowhAirBnB accommodation.'

At the bottom of the stairs, Mrs Pargeter watched very closely as he keyed in the code that released the lock on the door. She had been working on her aptitude for remembering numbers.

One of the first surprises was a sea view. Mrs Pargeter had dozed off towards the end of the Out-Boot Car journey, so she wasn't entirely sure where they had ended up. Devon, she heard Gary say at some point, but she had had no idea that St Perpetua's was near the sea.

The space in which they found themselves seemed to have been hewn out of solid rock. Or maybe it was a natural cave, which had been adapted to make upmarket accommodation. The main room had the window along the whole of one wall. Doors on either side presumably led to bedrooms, bathrooms and other facilities. Since neither Short Head nor Athena Shimmings were visible, Mrs Pargeter assumed they were behind those doors, checking out their accommodation.

She noticed there the shaft and doors of a protected dumb waiter, identical to those in the Safe Suite at Greene's Hotel. Maybe the same security designer had created both structures.

Truffler was thinking along the same lines. He asked Holy Smirke how the space had been converted.

'The cave's a natural one,' the vicar replied. 'Secret passages off it were built by the smugglers who operated here some time back. Direct access from the beach to the church. There's a vault beneath St Perpetua's which made a perfect storeroom for their brandy casks and what have you. Kept the goods away from the prying eyes of the Excise men.'

Reading disapproval in Mrs Pargeter's violet eyes, he said mischievously, 'The Church has always been a strong supporter of local industry.'

'Tell me, Holy,' said Truffler, 'who designed this lot? Because there's something about the place that has the style of an architect geezer Mr Pargeter used to work with. Oh, what was his name?'

'Derek the Draft,' Gary supplied.

'Presumably,' suggested Mrs Pargeter, 'he was called that because he was a good draftsman?'

'No,' said Holy Smirke. 'It was because he was dangerously fond of draught lager. But, actually, Truffler, you're right. Derek the Draft did design this. Did some work for Hedgeclipper Clinton at Greene's Hotel, I believe, as well.'

Mrs Pargeter smiled with the simple pleasure of being right.

'This place looks great,' said Gary. He was in a benign mood. The fates had, after all, granted him one of his most heartfelt desires – to spend the whole day in the company of Mrs Pargeter.

Truffler Mason raised a potential problem. 'That bloomin' great window looks good. Great view, but not so great security . . . From the sea it must be visible for miles.'

'Truffler,' said Holy Smirke, 'you underestimate Derek the Draft. That window is made of one-way glass. We can see out. No one can see in. And the other side of the glass is painted exactly to match the cliff face it looks out on.'

The private investigator nodded appreciatively. 'I get it. Very clever.'

At almost the same moment, doors on either side of the room opened to admit, respectively, Athena Shimmings and her son. The latter carried a laptop and had an urgent air about him. Truffler and Gary knew exactly why. At any time of the day or night, there's racing on somewhere. And where there's racing, there is of course the possibility of putting on a bet.

And the small matter of owing half a million to the Batinga Brothers wasn't going to stop Short Head Shimmings from doing what he reckoned he had been put on this earth to do. His motivation was simple, and common to all problem gamblers. This bet, as he'd told himself so many times before, is going to be the big win that makes up for all of those unfortunate losses in the past.

His mother, however, had different ideas. 'Put away that computer, Cecil,' she said, as she sat down in a comfortable armchair and gestured him to the one beside it. 'Now we have the opportunity to have a really nice long talk.'

The expression on her son's face, along with the wistful look at his laptop, showed how far having 'a really nice long talk' with his mother was from his ideal way of passing the time.

Ernestine's cassoulet lived up to its reputation. Her guests, having spent a long morning in the car after an early start, were more than ready for it. They were eating in the vicarage, a large, many-bedroomed building (those Victorian clergymen had so many children). The dining room featured bow windows, looking out across the graveyard to the Parish Church of St Perpetua the Martyr.

Truffler Mason drank beer. Mrs Pargeter, Ernestine and Holy shared an excellent bottle of his claret. Gary, for the usual professional reasons, stuck to the mineral water.

Their lunch party was joined by someone the London visitors hadn't met before, Ernestine's daughter Mignon. Lacking her parent's obvious flamboyance, she was a quietly attractive woman in her fifties. Though her mother was Frenchwoman thin, Mignon was built more on the comforting contours of Mrs Pargeter. She had no trace of a French accent, which suggested that she had been brought up in England.

This was confirmed by her mother, who kept up a constant barrage of criticism of her daughter throughout the lunch. For some reason of her own, she always referred to her in the third person.

'It is not natural, I think, for Mignon to be so subdued. She is a Frenchwoman, and Frenchwomen should do everything with éclat and panache. But I am afraid those English schools have injected too much of their national sangfroid into her veins.'

Mignon did not react. She had spent an entire lifetime listening to these gibes and they had become like water off the back of a canard.

Ernestine was not finished yet. 'A Frenchwoman is a woman of passion. Passion for life, passion for affaires, passion for sex! So why is it that my daughter always keeps so quiet about such matters?'

Possibly, thought Mrs Pargeter, because she's heard her

mother going on about them so much? But what she said was just a convenient way of diverting the conversation. 'I've often found with people that the more passionate they are about things, the less they talk about them. I mean, my late husband . . . no one could have been more dedicated to his work. And yet, did he ever say anything about it at home? Not a word.'

'He was a good man, Mr Pargeter,' announced Holy Smirke, in his best sermon voice. Truffler Mason and Gary agreed, nodding their heads in veneration. Mrs Pargeter caught a brief smile from Mignon, grateful for the support.

'So, what do you do here?' she asked.

'I am a cook,' Mignon replied. 'Not as good a cook as my mother –' Ernestine smiled at the compliment – 'but still pretty good.'

'Bloody marvellous cooks, both of them,' Holy Smirke asserted, patting his stomach which, Mrs Pargeter noticed, had expanded considerably since their previous encounter. 'Short Head and his mother couldn't be in more luxurious circumstances, even at Greene's Hotel.'

'So, Mignon,' Mrs Pargeter asked, 'you will actually be cooking for your NowhAirBnB guests, will you?'

'Yes, I look after them. Make sure that all their needs are catered for.'

'Well, Short Head's certainly landed on his feet, hasn't he? Have you met him yet, Mignon?'

'Very briefly. Just after he arrived. He seemed very charming.'

Mignon's mother again found an opportunity to criticise. 'Yes, I'm sure he's very charming. But did you impress on him how charming you are? I imagine not. You've never had the natural Frenchwoman's skill of making the best of yourself.'

With a clergyman's knack for keeping the peace, Holy Smirke intervened. 'I'm sure Short Head will have no complaints about your daughter's cooking and care while he's in residence here.'

Mignon gave a shy smile. 'I will do my best for him.'

'Of course she will,' said Holy Smirke bonhomously. 'As I said, they couldn't be in better hands. Mignon's a good girl.'

'I'm sure she is,' said Mrs Pargeter. 'And what about you, Holy? Are you continuing to be a good man?'

He looked slightly discomfited as he asked, 'What exactly do you mean, Mrs Pargeter?'

'There have been times, I believe, when your behaviour has not matched the high standards demanded by your vocation.'

'Really?'

'Yes, Holy. Stop looking so innocent. When we last met, when you were in charge of St-Crispin-in-the-Closet, you revealed to me that you were not above helping yourself to the odd twenty from the collection bag.'

'Oh, Mrs Pargeter,' said Holy, 'the Church of England is a broad church, broad enough, I like to think, not to get involved in petty nitpicking. The member of the congregation who puts money into the collection is doing it to help the upkeep of the church – and surely that encompasses the upkeep of its vicar. My taking twenty pounds from the collection merely speeds the process up, cutting out a few ecclesiastical middlemen along the way.'

'Hm.' Mrs Pargeter was not convinced. 'I always think you should be a Catholic priest, Holy, rather than an Anglican vicar. Your way of justifying unpalatable things would make any Jesuit jealous.'

He thanked her profusely, taking her words as a compliment. Which, in a way, they had been.

'And your direct line to God is still intact?'

'Certainly is,' he said with a grin. 'Never too busy to talk to me, God.'

'And what do you talk about?'

'Varies, Mrs P.'

'Do you discuss your guilty conscience about your past, Holy?'

'Funny, that subject never comes up.' The clergyman smiled beatifically to his assembled guests. 'No, I'm very fortunate. God's opinions on most matters do generally coincide with my own.'

The line was greeted by appreciative laughter, which Mrs Pargeter did not join in with. She knew Holy Smirke wasn't joking. He meant what he said. Isn't faith a wonderful thing, she thought to herself.

'One detail that I haven't been told,' he went on, 'and I'm fully prepared to remain in ignorance if that is appropriate, is who Short Head Shimmings and his mother are being protected from.'

Truffler Mason and Gary exchanged looks, questioning whether they should spill the beans. On a nod from the chauffeur, the private investigator replied, 'It's the Batinga Brothers.'

The smile left Holy Smirke's face, and he shuddered as though he had received a physical blow.

'Holy, are you all right?' asked Ernestine. Mignon looked equally anxious. Clearly, she also cared for her mother's partner.

The vicar recovered himself. 'Yes, yes, I'm fine,' he managed to say. 'Sorry, it's just, those names . . . they bring up memories from the past . . . memories I'd rather not think about.'

'I'm sorry,' said Mrs Pargeter, instantly solicitous. 'I thought you'd already know about who it was.' She looked anxiously at Truffler. 'We're not putting Holy and the others in danger, are we?'

He reassured her that wasn't the case. HRH would have set up surveillance around St Perpetua's and no harm could possibly come to Holy Smirke. Or Ernestine. Or Mignon. 'And no one on earth could break into where Short Head's hidden.'

'I'm glad to hear that,' said Mrs Pargeter with some relief. 'But you know what it means, don't you, Truffler?'

'What?'

'It means we can't waste any time in the business of dismantling the Batinga Brothers criminal empire.'

'You're right, Mrs P,' said Truffler, trying – and failing – to sound confident. The looks he exchanged with Gary and Holy weren't very optimistic either.

Somehow, the mention of their enemies' names had diluted the congeniality of the occasion. Ernestine's world-beating cassoulet had been followed by a world-beating plateau de fromage and a world-beating clafoutis aux cerises. These were eaten with minimal conversation.

And when, after coffee, Gary looked at his watch and said they ought to be on their way if they were to get back to Greene's Hotel in time for dinner, no one made any demur.

Though Mrs Pargeter herself obviously knew no details of the Batinga Brothers' crimes, the others in the car with her were all too aware of the monumental task that lay ahead of them.

Hedgeclipper Clinton provided them with a suitably lavish spread when they returned to his hotel. He asked if Mrs Pargeter wanted to take advantage of the suite that was always held in readiness for her, but she said she'd rather get home to Chigwell. 'That is, if you don't mind even more driving, Gary.'

'No worries, Mrs P,' said the chauffeur.

'But, I mean, you have just driven to Devon and back.'

'Like I say, Mrs P, no worries.'

'Well, if you're sure . . .'

Gary was sure. Though no one would ever know, what he had just been offered was the opportunity to spend another hour in the company of the woman he adored.

FIVE

'Jukebox' Jarvis – he got called that 'because he kept the records' – was sadly deceased, but his daughter Erin had taken over as archivist for the late Mr Pargeter's business dealings. And she had totally transformed the system. Though her father had experimented with the primitive computers of his time, he relied more on a random collection of dusty boxes, full of faded photocopies and grubby file cards. These his daughter had digitised, so that all that cumbersome paperwork was now contained on one sleek laptop.

Erin Jarvis looked pretty sleek too, the morning after Mrs Pargeter's trip to Devon. She was dressed in a well-cut charcoal-grey business suit, whose pinstripes were about six inches apart. Her hair had been well cut too, asymmetrically, like a purple hat on a slant.

And, as ever, she had found the exact information required by her guests, Mrs Pargeter and Truffler Mason. She had also supplied them with excellent coffee.

Erin read from her screen. 'The origins of the Batinga Brothers – named Damone and Como – have been deliberately shrouded in mystery. Their background – and even whether that is their real name – has never been satisfactorily established. All that is known is that, some thirty years ago, they became a dangerous presence in the East London underworld, with an empire stretching a good way into Essex, too.

'A series of daring raids on banks and building societies were soon being attributed to them. They were unpopular, not only with the police, but also with rival gangs whose turf they invaded. And, unlike other gangsters of the time, they never became folk heroes among the East End locals. The chief reason for this was the extreme cruelty displayed in their operations. In achieving their ends, the brothers didn't care who got hurt.

'As the Batingas became more successful, they recruited

muscle from other gangs, particularly Albanians and Romanians, but the principal figures remained Damone and Como Batinga, who were believed actually to be genuine brothers. Damone was the more cultured of the two, expensively suited, lover of expensive restaurants and flashy women. Whereas his brother Como had no finer feelings about anything. He was basically a sadistic psychopath.

'An interesting detail about Como . . . may sound trivial but in certain situations it can be important . . . he needs his sleep.'

'What?' asked a puzzled Mrs Pargeter.

'As I say,' Erin explained, 'he's a sadistic psychopath all the time. That's his default setting. But lack of sleep makes him even more sadistic and psychopathic. So, Mrs Pargeter, should you ever be so unfortunate as to be confronted by Como Batinga . . . and I hope that's a situation that never arises . . . just hope that it's on a day when he's had a good night's sleep.'

'I heard that about him, too,' Truffler contributed. 'Geezer I knew got the wrong side of him, day after Como had been up all night with the toothache.' He winced at the recollection. 'Not pretty it wasn't, not pretty at all.'

'Well,' said Mrs Pargeter, 'thank you. I'll bear that in mind.' Though being alone with a sleep-deprived Como Batinga was not a scenario that she envisaged ever happening to her. 'Go on, Erin, let's have more dirt on the Batingas.'

'Right you are, Mrs P. With the passage of the years, the Batinga Brothers moved on from raiding banks and building societies to more sophisticated levels of crime. Their activities expanded into areas of drug dealing, people trafficking, prostitution and loan sharking. The last of those now seems to be their main business. The London underworld still shudders at stories of the amounts people borrow from the Batinga Brothers, and the punishments that the Batinga Brothers administer to those who are slow to pay.

'Como Batinga is particularly inventive in that area. Nothing he likes better than devising tortures for adversaries who the brothers feel deserve correction. And when someone's held hostage to encourage the payment of a debt, he's very handy with a pair of wire-cutters. They're his weapon of choice. It's amazing how quickly people pay up after taking delivery of a severed ear or little finger belonging to a loved one.'

Mrs Pargeter thought it was probably just as well that Short Head Shimmings wasn't there to hear this. Though he probably knew quite enough about the reputation of the individuals he'd got the wrong side of.

Erin continued, 'Though they've been suspects for many crimes, neither Batinga brother has ever been convicted of any offence. This situation is attributed to the fact that they employ extremely expensive lawyers and, according to gangland rumour, have, over the years, greased a few willing palms in the Met.

'Like a lot of gangsters, Damone and Como Batinga have worked hard to separate themselves from the sharp end of villainy. They now work out of London offices from which they run a respectable property business. Damone is even a member of one of the City livery companies. Though there is no doubt that they are still the instigators of many major crimes in the capital and elsewhere – their global reach is extending by the day – it is a long time since either of them has been present at the scene of a crime. Every operation is carried out by thugs controlled through a complex network of intermediaries. As with the Mafia boss known as 'The Teflon Don', nothing is allowed to stick to either Batinga brother.

'These days, when violence is required, someone else does it for them . . . though maintaining that situation is not always easy. There are times when curbing Como Batinga's natural instinct for hurting people makes considerable demands on Damone and the rest of their respectable inner circle.

'Though they have less of a profile these days – due to skilful media manipulation – the profits of the Batinga Brothers' criminal enterprises have never been higher.'

Erin looked around at her guests. 'That's the outline,' she said. 'I can provide a lot more detail if you like.'

'No, I think that's fine. For the moment,' said Mrs Pargeter. 'They don't sound the kind of people you'd want to meet on a dark night, do they?'

Truffler and Hedgeclipper giggled uneasily.

'Still, we now at least know what we're up against, don't we?' Mrs Pargeter went on, cheerful as ever.

'Yes,' Truffler Mason agreed mournfully. 'Though Hedgeclipper and I have known that for quite a while. The question is: what should be our next step?'

'Well, that's obvious, isn't it?'

'Is it?'

'We set up a meeting with the Batinga Brothers, don't we?'

Mrs Pargeter beamed. Truffler Mason and Hedgeclipper Clinton did their best to mirror her expression, but the best they could come up with were extraordinarily watery smiles.

Gary, who'd been waiting outside Erin's in one of his Bentleys, drove Mrs Pargeter back to Chigwell. She sat in the front seat and chattered away blithely, little knowing the ecstatic experience she was providing for the man beside her.

'You got any young lady on the stocks at the moment, Gary?' she asked.

'No, no, nothing serious.'

'Well, you ought to have someone. Good-looking boy like you.'

She had no idea how much her compliment was appreciated, as he responded, 'I mean, I've been a bit cautious around women, you know, since my marriage broke up.'

'Yes, but that was a while back, wasn't it?'

'It was.'

'So, you really ought to be back in the market now. It's selfish, you know, Gary.'

'How'dja mean?'

'Well, depriving some poor girl of the pleasure of your company. And I think everyone's life's better with a bit of sex in it.'

Intrigued though he was at what she said, he didn't ask whether her life had got 'a bit of sex' in it. He thought probably the relationship she'd had with the late Mr Pargeter had been so perfect that she'd never made any attempt to replicate it. (And, in fact, he was right.)

'No, but, young man like you . . .' she persisted. 'I'm sure you have the capacity to make some woman very happy. So, you're not only depriving yourself, you're depriving this poor woman.'

'Maybe . . .'

'There's no "maybe" about it, Gary. I'm sure you've got as big a libido as the next man.'

'Well . . .'

'And you should take it out for a run sometime. I mean, otherwise, it's like having a Lagonda in your garage and never driving it.'

Gary just grunted. He had actually got two real Lagondas in his garage.

'Unless, of course,' Mrs Pargeter suggested, 'there already is someone in your life, someone you're holding a candle for, but who, for some reason, is not responding to your overtures. Or who, perhaps, is totally unaware of your feelings for her. Is there someone like that in your life?'

'Good heavens, no,' Gary lied, as he drove the Bentley on towards Chigwell.

After Mrs Pargeter and Gary drove off, Truffler Mason and Hedgeclipper Clinton had taken a cab back to Greene's Hotel.

'Do you think she really doesn't know?' asked Hedgeclipper anxiously.

'Always hard to tell with Mrs P,' came the lugubrious reply.

'Surely she must remember?'

'You'd have thought so, wouldn't you, Hedgeclipper? Mind you, Mr Pargeter was very good at keeping her out of the loop on anything to do with his work.'

'I know, but even so . . . Can't be many people who met the Batinga Brothers and completely forgot about it.'

'Mm. Mrs P's the exception to so many rules. Maybe she's the exception to that one, and all.'

Hedgeclipper shook his head. 'I mean, Truffler, it must have been a very traumatic experience for her, mustn't it?'

'It would have been for most people.'

'Unless, of course,' the hotelier suggested, 'she didn't know it was the Batinga Brothers she was dealing with . . .?'

'Possible, I suppose,' said Truffler. 'But surely very unlikely.'

'And now she's asking us to set up a meeting with the Batinga Brothers . . . There's no way we can do that, is there?'

'I don't think it'd be a great idea,' said a doom-struck Truffler. 'On the other hand, we have to be careful about how we prevent it from happening.'

'How'dja mean?'

'Hedgeclipper me old mate, as you know, Mrs Pargeter is a very determined woman. If we refuse to help her set up a meeting with the Batingas, she's quite capable of doing it off her own bat.'

'But does she have the contacts to do that?'

'You'd be surprised at the range of contacts Mrs Pargeter's got. Don't forget, Mr Pargeter bequeathed his little black book to her.'

Hedgeclipper Clinton nodded ruefully. 'I'd forgotten that.'

'So, if she can't get help in setting up a Batinga Brothers meeting from the obvious people – i.e. you and me – she wouldn't have a problem finding other of her late husband's associates to do the job for her.'

'Take your point, Truffler.'

'I think then, if she can't be persuaded against the idea of a meeting with the Batingas . . . it might be better if we were to set it up for her, rather than bringing in someone else.'

'And, that way, we could, like, protect her?'

'That's what Mr Pargeter asked us to do. On his deathbed. Wasn't it, Hedgeclipper?'

'It certainly was.' The hotelier looked pensive. 'I still have difficulty believing she genuinely can't remember what happened.'

'Well,' said Truffler Mason dolefully, 'we are talking thirty years ago, aren't we?'

SIX

Thirty years before that conversation between Truffler Mason and Hedgeclipper Clinton had taken place, Melita and Lionel Pargeter had just celebrated their first wedding anniversary. She was blissfully content with her lot. She couldn't imagine a more enchanting situation than that of being 'Mrs Pargeter'.

A happy marriage is difficult to describe, but those who've been lucky enough to participate in one know what it's like. (And, for those who haven't, a detailed description would only give rise to jealousy.)

However long a couple have known each other, however long they have cohabited, there is still something different about being married. Partly, it's the public statement of intent involved. But, also, there's the business of *really* getting to know each other. And, in a happy marriage, the more you find out about your partner, the better you like them.

It should also be said that, in a happy marriage, the sex is wonderful.

This was the good fortune of Melita and Lionel Pargeter. Having lived at varied addresses during his varied life, before the wedding Mr Pargeter had bought a well-appointed three-bedroomed detached house in Epping, near the famous forest. He had allowed his fiancée to choose all of the interior fittings and so Melita could say, in all honesty, that she had her 'dream house'. And whenever she asked him to sanction some expensive purchase, he came back with the encouraging words, 'Don't bother asking me, my love. Just buy it. I don't want you to worry your pretty little head about money.'

Some women, of a feminist persuasion, might have found this remark demeaning. Melita Pargeter, entirely confident of her gender and comfortable in her own skin, just knew when she was well off.

There were other things Lionel Pargeter didn't want his wife to 'worry her pretty little head' about. Aware how tedious financial details could be, he didn't burden her with information about where, specifically, their income came from. All she needed to know was that there was plenty of it.

Also, aware how boring men who were always talking about their jobs could be, he never brought work home with him. He had the enviable skill of completely compartmentalising what he did during the day from what he did with Melita in the evenings at the house in Epping. Long before the expression became fashionable, Mr Pargeter had achieved the perfect 'work/life balance'.

His work was undoubtedly demanding, and Melita was always ready to relax him when he returned from a particularly stressful assignment. Frequently, he would have to be away overnight, sometimes for a few nights in a row. But Mrs Pargeter never worried about what he got up to on these excursions. She was far too secure in their love to worry about any attractions other women might hold for him.

She was a good cook and always ready to prepare some delicious feast when he came home, but he rarely called on those talents. 'You don't want to mess about in the kitchen, Melita,' he would say. 'Let's go out. I want to show off my beautiful wife in public, don't I?'

There were a variety of pubs and restaurants that they frequented in the Epping area. And there were a couple, where Mr Pargeter had made arrangements with the owners, where his wife would be 'safe' to go on her own. Increasingly, on the evenings when her husband was working, Mrs Pargeter would take advantage of that facility. Eating out, she felt, was always more fun than eating in. And she had never minded enjoying a lavish, pampering meal on her own.

The issue of 'safety' was one that Mr Pargeter took very seriously. For the security of the Epping house, he had called on the talents of the best burglar alarm expert in the business. He was called 'Tumblers' Tate, the nickname deriving from the days before everything went electronic, back when all locks contained tumblers. And there was no sequence of tumblers that could deny the invasive skills of Tumblers Tate's picklocks.

Though Mr Pargeter had met Tumblers through work, he did not tell his wife that. It was yet another example of his belief in the economy of knowledge. Nobody should ever be burdened with more information than was absolutely essential. Brains, in his belief, had a finite capacity and one should be careful about what they were filled with.

Melita took his word for it that Tumblers Tate was the best in the business. Which he was. To know where her husband had met him would not have been relevant, just cluttering her mind with superfluous facts.

The security system Tumblers installed in the Epping house was a masterpiece. Sensors on all the doors and windows were connected to a computerised control box, whose number codes were automatically changed twice a day. It was a set-up which, in the words of Tumblers Tate himself, 'would have given Houdini a sick headache.'

The installation of the alarms took a surprisingly long time. When Mrs Pargeter asked why this was, her husband replied, 'Because only the best will do for you, my love. You are my most precious possession, and I want there to be no danger of your being nicked by some villain.'

Melita was charmed by the compliment. (Lionel omitted to mention that the house contained a lot of other precious possessions that he didn't want to be nicked by some villain either.)

Mrs Pargeter had an easy way with people and, while Tumblers Tate was working in the house, she supplied endless cups of tea ('Three sugars, love – I'm not sweet enough already.') and chatted to him.

He was one of those gnarled characters who it was difficult to put an age to. 'But,' he said, 'I been around the block a few times before I started working for your hubby. First job we ever done together was the NatWest in Billericay.'

'What – you set up their security system, did you?'

Tumblers chuckled. 'No such luck. Coo, if the banks allowed

me to do that for them, it'd make our job very easy, wouldn't it?'

Mrs Pargeter smiled with charming incomprehension.

'Next thing, Her Majesty's Prisons'll be letting us design their security systems, and all.' He chortled at the incongruity of the idea.

Out of politeness, Mrs Pargeter laughed along.

'He's a good boss, your hubby,' Tumblers went on.

'I'm sure he is,' Mrs Pargeter agreed.

'Honest,' he said. 'That's what counts in this caper.'

'I'm sure it does.'

'Don't want to work with geezers who're going to suddenly turn round and stab you in the back, do you?'

'No, you certainly don't.'

'There's a few of them around in our business,' said a ruminative Tumblers Tate. 'And what's more, they stab you with real knives!'

He laughed again and, once more, Mrs Pargeter laughed along. Though she really hadn't a clue what he was on about.

It was an evening in April, one of those pleasant evenings after British Summer Time has started, whose warmth brings the promise that summer is approaching. Business had taken Mr Pargeter away for three nights on the trot and his wife was very much looking forward to his return. They had fixed to meet in a restaurant, where they would have a very self-indulgent dinner, before going back to the Epping house for delicious, restorative sex.

As always, she dressed up for the occasion, wearing a pink off-the-shoulder shirtwaister dress with ruffles, which showed off her splendid bosom to advantage. Mr Pargeter, she knew, would be in his uniform of smart suit and tie. (He did not possess any leisurewear, though his wardrobe contained a wide range of different suits and ties.)

Apart from nominating the ones where he was sure his wife could go safely on her own, Mr Pargeter had other criteria for judging restaurants. He was temperamentally at odds with the concept of nouvelle cuisine, which had a minor vogue at the time. 'Pay through the nose for a couple of rabbit droppings and a squidge of sauce under a silver dome? I should cocoa,' he was frequently heard to comment. 'I like to see on the plate what I'm paying all that money for.'

As a result, the restaurants he favoured for tête-à-tête dinners with his wife were more traditional ones where the size of the portions matched their levels of cholesterol. A particular favourite was a venue in Theydon Bois called Triggers. Mr Pargeter knew the owner, Lennie, very well indeed and, because of some philanthropic act he had done for the welfare – or, more accurately, the security – of the restaurant, he was never presented with a bill at the end of a meal. (The same deal applied when Mrs Pargeter was dining there on her own.)

The Pargeters were always led by Lennie to the same table. Red cloth at the centre of which a lit candle stood proud above the drips left by many previous candles, descending in an immobile cascade to the top of the Chianti bottle's straw casing. Though they knew the menu by heart, they still enjoyed the process of consulting the atlas-sized cardboard folder. They opened the paper envelopes of grissini breadsticks, dipped them into full-fat butter and munched away as they perused what was on offer.

These were the glory days, when only faddists counted calories (a habit which, throughout her life, Mrs Pargeter had never grown into). The starters included Minestrone Soup, French Onion Soup, Prawn Cocktail, Devilled Eggs and, for those wanting a spurious feeling of being virtuous, Tropical Fresh Fruit Cocktail au Kirsch.

Moving on to the mains, the Pargeters would read through the list of available fare, which encompassed Chicken Kiev, Boeuf Stroganoff, Duck à l'Orange, Steak Rossini, Steak au Poivre, Steak Diane, Chicken Cordon Bleu, Beef Wellington, Coronation Chicken, Hunter's Chicken, Chicken Curry and Chips, Poulet Roti Fermière, Salmon en Croute and Surf 'n' Turf. The last item was Lobster and Filet Mignon for those who liked to make their consumption particularly conspicuous. (And there were quite a few such people in the Epping area.)

Later in the meal, when Lennie asked if they wanted a

dessert, Mrs Pargeter would always say, 'Oh, well, I'll just have a look at the menu.' And always end up having one. Because what was on offer included Black Forest Gâteau, Queen of Puddings, Bakewell Tart, Sticky Toffee Pudding, Baked Alaska, Lemon and Sultana Cheesecake and Charlotte Rousse.

Then, of course, after the desserts, there was a list of 'Speciality Coffees'. Of these, Triggers offered Irish, Russian, Parisian, Calypso, Caribbean, Highland and Brazilian.

Needless to say, while they perused the menu, the Pargeters had already been supplied with cocktails. They weren't asked about these. Their order was always the same – a Garibaldi (Campari, Orange Juice and Ice) for Mr Pargeter and a Snowball (Advocaat, Lime, Lemonade and Ice) for his lovely wife.

After all the ritual menu scrutiny, Lennie would come to take their order. With important guests, this was a duty he always fulfilled himself. Efficient though his team of waitresses were, he knew where respect was due.

The Pargeters would give their orders and the restaurateur would write them down on his pad . . . though he had written exactly the same words on the sheet last time they came to Triggers . . . and the time before . . . and the time before that . . .

They would both go for the Prawn Cocktail starter, but thereafter their tastes diverged. Mrs Pargeter always selected the Duck à l'Orange and her husband went for the Steak Diane. This was because he enjoyed the theatre of having the steak flambéed at the table. He would watch with undiminished delight as the meat was seared and covered with cream and mushroom sauce. Then, when the dish was placed in front of him, he would religiously scrape off all the sauce before eating it. It was an unchanging ritual that gave him great pleasure.

Having committed their menu choices to paper, Lennie would then ask, 'And to drink . . .?'

The responses here were predictable, too. 'Well, we'd better have a couple more of these cocktails,' Mr Pargeter would say. 'Then, with our starters, we'll have a bottle of the Promiscuous Girl.'

'"Promiscuous Girl"?' Lennie would echo, exactly as if he hadn't heard the joke before. Many times.

'I mean the old Blue Nun,' Mr Pargeter would say, timing his punchline, 'because that *goes with everything*!' (Blue Nun was a German Liebfraumilch, much drunk at the time. It vied for popularity with Mateus Rosé, a medium-sweet frizzante wine from Portugal. Rumour had it that ignorant English customers, unable to decide between red and white wine, would say, 'Well, let's have a bottle of the old Mateus Rosé.' Because that, like Blue Nun, was thought to 'go with everything'.)

Lennie would grant Mr Pargeter's joke an appropriate laugh, as he had done every other time he'd heard it.

Then Mrs Pargeter would intercede. Though it was not in her nature to go against the wishes of her husband, she did find the Blue Nun a little sweet and sticky for her taste. So, she made sure, of course in the most charming and unthreatening manner, that she was the one who decided about which wine they would drink with their main courses.

As a rule, Mrs Pargeter favoured red. And Mr Pargeter, having got through the Blue Nun, would be happy to have red with his steak. So, from the Triggers' wine list, she selected a bottle of Le Piat d'Or, possibly influenced by the television ad campaign whose strapline was: 'The French adore Le Piat d'Or' (though no self-respecting French wine drinker would have gone near the stuff).

Their second Garibaldi and Snowball having been delivered, they drank them with relish while awaiting the arrival of their starters. They talked of this and that. Another feature, they both knew, of a happy marriage was never to run out of conversation and, equally, not to worry about occasional silences. A relationship in which you can comfortably sit together without saying anything is one to be treasured. As ever, between the two of them no subjects were off limits . . . except, of course, Mr Pargeter's work.

Mrs Pargeter could not be unaware that evening that, after they had given their orders, her husband seemed a little preoccupied. Usually, when he was with her, he had eyes for nobody else. But on this occasion, she was aware of his gaze straying to focus on something behind her. Deploying the old trick of dropping her table napkin and reaching round to pick it up, she was able to see what was attracting his attention.

It must have been the couple at the table behind her, who hadn't been there when the Pargeters arrived. A tall man with jet-black hair had his besuited back to her, but she got a full view of his companion. She was young, maybe not even twenty, thin but with unfeasibly large breasts. Her hair had been recently styled in a feathered mushroom cut as favoured by Princess Diana. She wore a purple sequinned power suit with huge padded shoulders. If she stood up, Mrs Pargeter thought, the girl would have the outline of an inverted slice of cake.

The napkin retrieved, she once again sat, facing her husband. Though the young woman was undoubtedly attractive, the thought never occurred to her that that might be the reason for Mr Pargeter's interest. Mrs Pargeter felt unshakably secure in her own relationship and her own attractiveness. She didn't need shoulder pads to make her feel powerful. The knowledge that she was powerful came naturally to her.

She somehow knew it wasn't the moment to ask Mr Pargeter who the couple he recognised were, but she didn't have to wait long for all to be revealed. She saw her husband's eyes raised as the man behind her got up from his seat and, accompanied by Lennie, approached their table.

The restaurateur said, 'Mr Smith . . .'

To her surprise, Mr Pargeter responded, 'Yes, Lennie?'

'I think you have already met Mr Smith.' Lennie gestured to the man standing beside him. What Mrs Pargeter could now see was a tall dark-haired man, who would have been good-looking had his face been narrower and his jaw less shield-shaped. As it was, he looked like a cartoon of someone good-looking. His suit had a sharkskin sheen to it, as well as too many pockets in the jacket. And the tie with silver and mauve stripes over a shiny scarlet shirt had not been a judicious fashion choice. Mrs Pargeter congratulated herself on how much better her husband's dress sense was. Mr Pargeter's sober pinstripe and tie in two shades of blue was much more discreet and stylish.

The pause went on a little longer than was comfortable. Lennie bridged the silence by saying heartily, 'I always think it's funny that you're both called Smith.'

'Very funny,' said Mr Pargeter.

'Hilarious,' said the other Mr Smith.

'When one of you phones to book, the girls don't know which one it is,' Lennie floundered on. 'They have to get me to the phone, because I recognise your voices.'

'I'm sure they do,' said Mr Pargeter.

'Undoubtedly,' said the other Mr Smith.

'Well, I, um . . .' Lennie looked desperately across the room, where nobody was summoning him. 'Just got to check something in the kitchen,' he said as he scuttled away.

The two Mr Smiths looked at each other.

'It's not often that we are granted the pleasure of meeting socially,' said the other Mr Smith, the words coming out heavy as gravestones.

'No,' Mr Pargeter agreed. 'It's more often that we meet antisocially.'

The tall man turned his gaze on to his acquaintance's companion. 'And you, a process of elimination dictates, must be the lovely Mrs Pargeter.'

'Yes.' She smiled graciously. 'My name's . . .' Reacting to a quick shake of the head from her husband, she concluded lamely, 'Mrs Pargeter.'

'How delightful to have the pleasure of meeting you at last.'

She didn't quite understand the 'at last' but asked, nodding towards the woman still seated at the other table, 'Are you going to introduce us to your—?'

'No,' the other Mr Smith interrupted. 'She doesn't matter.'

Mrs Pargeter was getting a little anxious about the atmosphere between the two Mr Smiths beginning to seethe, but relief appeared in the form of a waitress carrying their two Prawn Cocktails. These were served in conical glasses, standing on plates which bore the Triggers logo of two crossed revolvers.

The other Mr Smith realised that the arrival of the Pargeters' food was his cue to depart. 'It's been a pleasure to make your acquaintance, Mrs Pargeter,' he said. And then, again, the bizarre addition, 'At last.'

He turned to her husband. 'I'm sure, by the same token, with the inevitability of such things, that our paths will cross again before too long, Mr Smith,' he said.

'I'm sure they will,' said Mr Pargeter drily, 'Mr Smith.'

The other Mr Smith returned to his table.

The encounter didn't exactly spoil their evening, but it made the start of it less relaxed than usual. Fortunately, the other Mr Smith did not stay long.

Mrs Pargeter could not see but, very soon after his conversation with Mr Pargeter ended, having downed his cocktail and not even given a food order, the tall man stood up, took his companion by the hand and dragged her out of the restaurant. She objected with some vigour to this treatment. 'You said we was going to have a proper night out, Damone. Not just go straight to bed like you usually make me.'

Hearing the girl's Essex squeals of complaint, Mrs Pargeter turned to witness the departure.

She looked back to see her husband considerably more at ease. She focused her violet eyes on him, silently questioning.

'Work thing,' Mr Pargeter said dismissively.

Mr Pargeter was careful about the law. He never wanted to get in a situation where he might inadvertently have broken it. So, when they emerged from Triggers, his wife was not surprised to find there was a Bentley waiting for them outside. Her husband would never risk being done for driving under the influence.

The young, uniformed chauffeur, as he opened the back doors for them, looked with gobsmacked adulation at Mrs Pargeter. Little did she know – little did she ever know – that that moment had ignited in him a lifetime of adoration.

When he was back in the driving seat, he asked, 'Fast getaway, is it, Mr Pargeter?'

'No. Domestic speed, thank you, Gary.'

'Very good,' said the chauffeur.

'Incidentally, Lionel . . .'
'Yes, Melita my love?'
'Why did Lennie address you as "Mr Smith"?'
'Oh, I always book in that name. I ring and say to Lennie, "Table for two for Mr and Mrs Smith." Little joke between us. Like you and I was an adulterous couple.'

Mrs Pargeter would never have dreamed of asking him whether he'd ever needed to use that ploy in his previous life. Nor did the thought cross her mind that he might be making a suggestion to 'spice up' their love life. Their love life needed no 'spicing up'.

'But,' she said, 'Lennie referred to the other gentleman as "Mr Smith".'

'Yes. Coincidence, eh?'

'You know him, though, don't you?'

'I wouldn't say "know". I have met him briefly in a work connection.'

'So, in his case, "Smith" is his real name?'

'That's it,' Mr Pargeter lied.

After the Bentley eased its way through the lanes of Essex, Mrs Pargeter observed of their chauffeur, 'Very good driver, isn't he?'

'Oh yes,' said her husband. 'Trouble is . . .'

'What?'

'Gary's only fifteen,' said Mr Pargeter.

SEVEN

Though far-sighted and innovative in his professional life, in the domestic sphere Mr Pargeter had some quite old-fashioned ideas. For example, he was of the generation which believed that a wife going out to work was a reflection on her husband's inability to look after her properly. Which was a source of some frustration to Mrs Pargeter.

She was a woman who felt absolutely no guilt about being pampered. She could quite happily find things to do in the Epping house, while waiting to go out for the next meal. On the other hand, few of the time-filling activities beloved of other wealthy unemployed wives appealed to her. Comfortable in her own skin, she felt no need to be constantly titivating her body. She had found an excellent hairdresser, which was the most important bit and she visited him on a monthly schedule.

Otherwise, trusting what nature had blessed her with, she wore the minimum of make-up. And, as for body maintenance, it didn't interest her. She knew her husband worshipped every substantial contour of her, so why should she bother to make any changes?

'Going to the gym' was an increasingly popular trend at the time, but Mrs Pargeter had no wish to get unnecessarily sweaty. Nor did any of the other constantly extending range of spa treatments hold any allure for her. The semi-mystic disciplines of yoga and Pilates were equally unappealing.

Other idle wives filled their time with tennis or golf but she, whose serene personality contained no competitive element, could not see the attraction.

And, as for the idea of going on a diet . . . there was no way Mrs Pargeter was ever going to make herself feel guilty about a healthy enjoyment of eating and drinking.

But there was still a nurturing element in her personality

which required activation. She always wanted to be doing something that did someone good.

So, she discussed with her husband the ticklish subject of what constituted 'work'. Incidentally, though people in his world of business had found Mr Pargeter an uncompromising negotiator, she never had a problem getting her point across to him. And, though he terrified many in his professional life, such a reaction never entered her mind. She knew that, ultimately, she could always get round him. Though, in their relationship, she appeared infinitely biddable, she did in fact have a will of steel.

And she very quickly convinced her husband that 'work' was something you got paid for. So, he could therefore make no objection to anything she did for charity. Being of an entrepreneurial nature, Mrs Pargeter did not offer her services to any existing charity. She set up one of her own.

The nearest prison to their Epping house was HMP Romford. She arranged an interview with the governor to put forward her suggestion to him. She knew how busy the Parole Board always was and suggested that she could offer a follow-up service to help find work for prisoners after their release. The governor was impressed both by her and by the idea.

When Mr Pargeter heard of the plan, his first anxiety was for his wife's safety, but she reassured him that the initial sessions she conducted with her clients would be on HMP Romford's premises, under strict prison security. She didn't mention how she was going to proceed after those initial sessions, but fortunately, her husband hadn't asked that question.

All he said was: 'Mixing with the criminal element, eh? Well, rather you than me, Melita.'

The first meeting she set up was in a small interview room at HMP Romford. A prison officer was present, but his laid-back attitude suggested he didn't anticipate any trouble from the inmate Mrs Pargeter was talking to.

She, too, was impressed by what a gentle man he was. Huge and muscular but very gentle. The officer introduced him as Mr Jacket. 'But everyone calls me "Concrete",' he said.

'Hello, Concrete,' said Mrs Pargeter. 'I gather you're to be released soon.'

'Yes,' he agreed gloomily. 'Until the next time.'

'That doesn't sound very optimistic.'

'It's realistic,' he said ruefully. 'I don't know, I do seem to have a lot of bad luck.'

'I'm sorry to hear that.'

'Just seems to happen to me. I mean, this latest stretch I done . . . I'm a builder, that's my trade. And how was I to know that the geezer who was offering me a load of bricks at a really good price . . . he'd only nicked them from an Essex County Council storage yard in Basildon?'

'You couldn't have known, could you?'

'No. So, the fact that I bought them in good faith, does that cut the mustard in court? Does it hell? So, I'm down for six months, aren't I?'

'And, Concrete, you say this keeps happening to you?'

'Yes. And I'm engaged . . . and I've got this lovely fiancée called Tammy . . . and we keep having to put off the wedding . . .'

'Because you keep being detained at Her Majesty's Pleasure?'

'That's it. You've won the coconut there, Mrs Pargeter.'

'May I just check, Concrete? Are you a sole trader or do you work for someone else?'

'Sole trader. And that brings its own problems. I've never been that hot on the paperwork, so I'm not the most popular geezer with the tax authorities. I've been sent down for that, and all.'

'And, Concrete, so far as you know, you've never actually committed a crime?'

'No. God's honour. All the stretches I done, they all been down to unfortunate misunderstandings. I'm a good builder – honest, Mrs Pargeter – but I have suffered a lot of bad luck.'

'It sounds as if you have,' she said, as sympathetically as if she believed him. 'I wonder if you might be better off working for someone else, where you don't have the problem of running the business side as well as doing the actual building work . . .?'

'That'd be great,' he responded enthusiastically. But gloom quickly returned as he said, 'But who's going to employ me, with a criminal record like I got?'

'Do you know, Concrete,' said Mrs Pargeter, 'I think I might have an answer to that.'

She raised the issue with her husband that evening over dinner at one of their favourite local hostelries. 'I know you don't like talking about your work, Lionel . . .'

He was instantly on his guard. 'For very good reasons, Melita.'

'Yes, I'm aware of that, my love. But I just wondered . . .'

'Yes?'

'Whether in the course of your work, you ever need the services of a builder?'

'It might possibly happen,' he replied cautiously.

'Because, through my charity work at HMP Romford, I came across a prisoner about to be released, who I believe is a really good builder. And he says he'll never get any more work because he'll have a criminal record. And I was thinking, you're such a naturally generous person, Lionel . . .'

'Mm?'

'That you wouldn't be prejudiced against someone because they had a criminal record.'

'No,' he agreed. 'It's very easy to get on the wrong side of the law.' He checked himself. 'Or so I have been told. And there are occasions in my work when I do need the services of a good, dependable builder. Give me the gentleman's contact details.'

Mrs Pargeter couldn't have been happier. To know that she and her husband would be effectively working together on her charity project. Maybe, between them, they would develop this recruitment service to help many more unfortunate men overcome the taint of criminality.

She felt blessed to be married to a man of such generosity.

There was a small café in Chipping Ongar which was called No Greens. The reason for the name was that everything served there was deep-fried and no vegetable other than a tomato had ever been allowed admittance to its kitchen.

The café was run by a gentleman called Mr Clinton. Nobody had ever found out his first name but everyone knew him as 'Hedgeclipper' Clinton. He had earned the nickname for the innovative ways in which, working for Mr Pargeter, he had on occasion used that particular garden tool.

One morning, a few months after employment had been found for Concrete Jacket, the builder's skills were being praised in No Greens Café. Gary, the getaway driver, was there, accompanied by a very tall, lugubrious young man, who also worked for Mr Pargeter. His surname was Mason and, in honour of his talent for finding out information that people didn't want found out – and, indeed, finding people who didn't want to be found – he was nicknamed 'Truffler'.

Hedgeclipper Clinton had just served his two customers with Full Englishes, just the way they liked them, swimming in grease, when Truffler observed, in his customarily doleful manner, 'Really good, that new builder Mr P has just taken on board.'

'Concrete Jacket? I'll say!' Gary agreed. 'Real master craftsman we got there.'

'Yeah,' said Hedgeclipper. 'Didn't he have a bit of a dodgy rep at one point, working for some really nasty types, proper gangsters?'

'I heard some rumour about that,' said Truffler. 'But he'll be all right now he's on Mr P's books.'

''Course he will,' said Hedgeclipper, reassured.

'Didn't Concrete Jacket build the tunnel to the Midland Bank offices in Braintree?' asked Hedgeclipper.

'He certainly did,' said Truffler Mason.

'Lovely job, that,' Gary agreed. 'Beautifully finished tunnel – and a trapdoor entrance straight into their vaults.'

'Concrete's good, the real deal,' said Truffler. 'He's as versatile as an egg.'

'Yes,' said Gary. 'Mr P was talking about getting him to build a safe room in their house in Epping.'

'Great idea!' said Truffler, with the deflated intonation which denoted enthusiasm. 'He'd do it sweet as a nut, no probs.'

'Sounds like we're lucky to have him on the team,' said

Hedgeclipper. Employees of Mr Pargeter were always generously appreciative of their colleagues' skills.

'Mr P's got the knack, hasn't he,' said Gary, 'of always finding the right person for a job?'

Truffler nodded. 'Recruitment skills, that's what it is.'

'Yeah, I wonder how he does it,' said Gary.

But none of them in the No Greens Café knew that he actually relied, for some of his recruitment, on the headhunting skills of his wife.

It was nearly a fortnight after the encounter between the two Mr Smiths in Triggers. The days were lengthening, raising that very English – but not borne out by experience – hope of a good summer. Maybe in anticipation of that, Mrs Pargeter was dressed in a smock-like Laura Ashley dress, with a pattern of white flowers on a green background. Mr Pargeter was away overnight on business, and his wife hadn't the energy to go out to eat.

People who did not know her might think that she would therefore be in the kitchen, preparing some simple but wholesome meal for one, maybe frugally using up remains of other meals from the fridge. People who did know her would be unsurprised to hear that she had, instead, ordered the Number Three Special Banquet for One from the local Chinese takeaway. She particularly liked this because it included three of her favourite dishes: Wonton Soup, Sweet and Sour Pork and Banana Fritters.

By the time the order arrived, she had opened a Châteauneuf du Pape and downed a glass in readiness. Though not given to alcoholic excess, it wouldn't surprise her if the bottle was empty by the end of the evening. And she'd got her knife and fork out on the kitchen table. She could never be fussed with the chopsticks that would arrive with the order.

Following Mr Pargeter's instructions, Tumblers Tate had installed a special security feature by the front door to facilitate safe deliveries. A screen would reveal who was standing outside and encourage them to identify themselves. If given the go-ahead, they would then place the goods in a bombproof tray, which would slide automatically inside the house. Once the contents had been retrieved, any required payment could be put in the tray and returned to the courier.

Mrs Pargeter considered at times that this level of security was unnecessarily high, but she didn't voice such feelings to her husband. She knew that all these precautions were expressions of his love. And surely it was better to be with someone who was overprotective than someone who didn't give a damn about her?

The Number Three Special Banquet for One having been delivered by the usual method, she went into the kitchen to enjoy her dinner. It seemed excessive to set a place for herself in the dining room. Mrs Pargeter could do formal when the occasion required it, but her natural instinct was for simplicity. In everything she did, she always went for comfort. Eating a Chinese takeaway at the kitchen table, with a nice bottle of Châteauneuf du Pape to hand, fulfilled all her requirements.

She didn't need the television on. Or the radio. Or background music. Just as she was secure in her own skin, so Mrs Pargeter was secure in her own thoughts.

She was sitting with her back to the hall door, so she was unaware of the intruders until they grabbed her. All she was aware of was something damp and sweet-smelling being pressed on to her nose and mouth before she lost consciousness.

EIGHT

When she came to, which was a slow process of repeatedly half-waking and slipping back into darkness, Mrs Pargeter found herself lying on a bed in a windowless room wallpapered in white. Her head ached but she couldn't blame the brightness of the lights. They were relatively subdued, one table lamp by the bed and a double sconce on the opposite wall.

Though she had presumably been bustled in there unconscious, she did not feel as if she had suffered any damage in transit. Still wearing the Laura Ashley dress she'd had on whenever she was last awake, she observed that someone had thoughtfully put a blanket over her. She wasn't tied up or handcuffed. She could move freely.

As the swoops back into oblivion became shorter, she thought she might have a go at standing up. Her head didn't share the opinion that that was a good idea. It felt detached from her body, waywardly rolling in some dimension of its own. It took a while, but she did manage to sit upright on the edge of the bed.

She looked at her watch. Three fifteen. Whether she'd been out for seven hours or nineteen she had no means of knowing. She made a more detailed scrutiny of the room. There were two grey doors, though she couldn't work out which was the one she'd been brought in through. On each there was a numbered keypad. Presumably, the right codes would let somebody in and out.

Even in her fuddled state, she registered the anomaly of there being a keypad on the inside of her prison door as well, presumably, as one on the outside. It suggested the room wasn't just used for purposes of incarceration. Some of its occupants must have been free to go in and out. Perhaps they were people who were being hidden away for their own protection.

She tried again to rise. Very unsteady on her feet, but she stayed upright. She moved gingerly towards one of the doors and tried the handle. It was firmly locked and, of course, she didn't have the code to open it.

She tottered across to the other door, which opened easily to reveal a bathroom. She had hoped she might find another exit in there, but there was no sign of one. The wall opposite was tiled in grey, around a white vanity unit. Above this was a mirror, for shaving or applying make-up.

Beside the basin was a neat basket of grey-packaged soap, shampoo and conditioner. Up on the wall, she noticed an extractor fan. For a second, she wondered whether this might offer a possible means of escape. But the hope was immediately extinguished. An emaciated Dickensian chimney sweep might have stood a chance of getting through the aperture when the fan was removed. But for her, with the ample curves so appreciated by Mr Pargeter . . . not a chance.

The carpet in the main room was grey. The sheets and duvet cover were white, the blanket again grey. There was no adornment of any kind on the walls, no ornaments on any surface. The lack of windows obviated the need for curtains. She was in a monochrome world.

Apart from the green of her Laura Ashley dress, the only colour came, incongruously, from a bowl of fruit on a table. A bowl of fruit, like the basket of bathroom goodies, as if she were an honoured guest in a hotel room.

But Mrs Pargeter was under no illusions. She wasn't in a hotel. She was in a prison.

As a rule, Mr Pargeter didn't do any business from the Epping house. It was off limits for his associates. But this time was different. He couldn't maintain the customary division between home life and work life. They had been crudely forced together. His home was now a crime scene.

So, when, the evening after her abduction, he came back from work to find his wife gone, he had no hesitation in summoning Truffler Mason and Hedgeclipper Clinton to the house.

According them the same respect most people – though possibly not Mr Pargeter – would have granted to the police, he did not touch anything in the house until his team had done their forensic analysis. The unfinished Number Three Special Banquet for One was still on the kitchen table, quietly congealed. The bottle of Châteauneuf du Pape was half-empty and uncorked, smelling vinegary by now.

Neither Truffler nor Hedgeclipper had undergone any official police instruction, beyond being told to get lost from various locations throughout their childhoods. But they had both acquired extensive policing skills, by methods of their own. And their abilities to collect information from a crime scene were at least as good as those of professional scene of crime officers.

Truffler tended to concentrate on fingerprints and Hedgeclipper on footprints. They worked together on carpet fibres, dust and other residues. Both were expert in reading bloodstains. They could quickly identify the weapon used to cause them and such other details as the height of the person wielding it.

Fortunately, that particular expertise was not required at the Epping house. Their examination of the scene suggested that no violence had been involved in the abduction of Mrs Pargeter. Though that news was comforting to her husband, it did not tell him enough. Knowing his wife's character, he wondered what inducement could have made her follow her captors without resistance.

Mr Pargeter had long experience of keeping his emotions under control and, in spite of the anxieties seething within, waited with apparent patience while his team completed their inspection.

Eventually, after a final re-examination of the delivery system by the front door, Truffler Mason and Hedgeclipper Clinton reported back to him in the kitchen.

'Very professional job,' said the tall one gloomily. 'Footprints suggest there were two of them but they covered their tracks very efficiently. Wore gloves, not a smidgeon of a fingerprint anywhere.'

'Signs of a break-in?'

Hedgeclipper shook his head. 'I've checked all possible access points, Mr Pargeter. Nothing.'

'Which means?'

Truffler replied, 'It means . . . that they came in through the front door. Which in turn means . . .'

'I know what it means, Truffler!' the boss snapped, on the edge of losing his cool. 'It means that whoever broke into the house had the codes for the security system.'

Truffler Mason nodded a lugubrious nod.

'Which also means that, since Tumblers Tate was the only person apart from me who knew those codes, either he has been put under pressure to reveal them . . .'

'Or?' asked Hedgeclipper Clinton, with the weariness of someone who knew what was coming.

'He's gone over to the other side!'

'So,' asked Truffler, 'what do you want us to do?'

'Find Tumblers Tate!' said Mr Pargeter. 'But, more important than that, find my wife!'

After exploring the dimensions of her prison, Mrs Pargeter lay back on the bed. Whatever had knocked her out was still heavy in her system and she slipped back into sleep.

She was wakened by the sound of something being pushed under the locked door. She rose unsteadily and bent down – not a comfortable manoeuvre with a head like hers – to pick it up.

A menu, with boxes to be ticked by the customer for their meal selections. Again, more in keeping with a hotel than a prison.

The fare on offer was not as exciting as Mrs Pargeter might have wished, but at least it suggested her captors were not planning to starve her to death. The fact that it was a lunch menu might suggest it was now more likely to be nearly four in the afternoon than four in the small hours.

Using a pen that she found next to the bowl of fruit, she ticked the boxes for Tomato Soup, Roast Chicken and Sherry Trifle, then, head swimming as she once again bent down, pushed the menu back under the door.

Maybe the person outside had been waiting for the signal that she was awake, because the door opened immediately, to reveal a short man who had the face and aggressive stance of a boxer. A boxer dog, that is, though he did have some qualities of an old-fashioned prize fighter, too. Perhaps aware of his clumsy appearance, he stepped daintily into the room, closing the door behind him.

'So,' he said, 'you are the famous Mrs Pargeter.'

'I don't know about "famous",' she said, unfazed by his sudden arrival.

'The way my brother talks about you, you are famous.'

'Do I know your brother?' she asked with some hauteur.

'He says he met you in Triggers.'

'Ah. Mr Smith.'

The musclebound man chuckled. 'If you like. Mr Smith.'

'So, if you're his brother, you must also be Mr Smith.'

He found that even funnier. 'Yes, all right. Como Smith, that's my name.'

'And your brother's name is Damian.'

'Dam*one*,' he corrected her, extending the second syllable unnaturally.

'And which one of you do I have to thank for abducting me in this very uncivilised manner?'

He thought about the question for a moment. 'I guess you could say both of us.'

'You both broke into my house in Epping and—?'

'No, no, we didn't actually do the break-in.' He added, with considerable pride, 'We have people to do that kind of stuff for us. We have people to do most things.'

Flamboyantly he opened a cupboard door to reveal shelves loaded with bubble-wrapped, sardine-tin-sized packages. 'We have people to sell these for us.'

'What are they?' asked Mrs Pargeter, thinking of the array of toiletries in the bathroom. 'Bars of soap?'

So far as Como was concerned, she had just cracked another great joke. When he had stopped laughing, he said, 'No, not bars of soap. That is the finest cocaine. Well, no, not the finest. We've had it cut with a few less fine ingredients to make it go further. But there's enough of the stuff there to keep the East End supplied for a good few weeks.'

Mrs Pargeter was appalled. 'Are you saying . . .' she asked with some trepidation, 'that you and your brother run a criminal gang?'

'That's right,' agreed the short man. 'And not just any criminal gang, either. We are the most successful criminal gang operating in the East End and Essex area. Hardened crooks go quiet when they hear our name. We are the most feared brothers around.'

'The Smith Brothers?' Mrs Pargeter almost sneered.

This suggestion caused him even more hilarity. 'Yes. "The Smith Brothers". Sounds pretty scary, huh?'

'Not to me it doesn't,' said Mrs Pargeter. If she was feeling any anxiety about her predicament, she was determined not to show it. And she was feeling considerable anxiety. The fact that Como Smith was so casually showing her the stash of cocaine meant he wasn't concerned about her ever testifying to the police about what she'd seen. Which in turn could suggest that he wasn't expecting her to leave her current confinement alive.

'Anyway,' she went on, 'maybe you'd be kind enough to tell me where I am.'

'You're in a secret place,' said Como.

'Quite possibly. But could you tell me *where*?'

'If I told you where, it wouldn't be so secret, would it?' came the sly response.

'Very well. Let me try another approach. *Why* am I here?'

'Ah.' He thought about this. 'Well, people who come here come here for one of two reasons.'

'That's not very helpful.'

'No. Maybe I should spell it out for you . . .?'

'That would be most kind,' said Mrs Pargeter primly.

'Some people,' he began slowly, 'come here because they've done something to upset us.'

'"Us" being the Smith Brothers?'

This seemed to amuse him more than ever. 'Exactly. And people who upset –' giggle giggle – 'the Smith Brothers . . .

tend to get punished. In those cases, this room is kind of a . . . holding cell, if you like . . . where they stay while we decide what punishment is most suitable for them.'

'That obviously doesn't apply to me,' said Mrs Pargeter serenely. 'Saying hello to your brother in Triggers can hardly constitute upsetting someone.'

'You can never be sure,' said Como. 'Damone is exceptionally sensitive to the smallest insult.'

'Well, I didn't insult him,' came the brisk response. 'So, what's the other reason why people are shut in here?'

'Ah. In some cases, people can be very useful as a means of persuasion.'

'What do you mean by that, Como?'

'Let us imagine a situation . . . Say, you've got a turf war going on . . . You know what a "turf war" is, Mrs Pargeter?'

One of her great abilities – which she deployed rarely – was to appear ignorant. 'I suppose so,' she replied. 'It seems an odd thing to go to war about, but I know gardeners can get obsessive. Not, incidentally, that I'm one of them. I think gardening's a weedy occupation.'

Como did a brief double-take at this response but continued spelling out his scenario. 'So, there's this turf war going on, and let us say one of the opposing gangs wants to put pressure on the other. And they ask themselves: have they got any weaknesses? Is there something that matters a lot to them? Something which, if it were stolen, they might pay a lot to get back?'

'A hostage is what you're saying?'

'If you like, Mrs Pargeter. To extend the example, let us say that . . . I don't know . . . Mr Pargeter perhaps. Say he was in dispute with me and my brother in a turf war . . .?'

'It's very unlikely,' she said, in all apparent innocence. 'He doesn't like gardening any more than I do.'

This prompted a snort of frustration from Como. 'Let's just say, for the sake of argument, that it happened. Someone Mr Pargeter cared a lot for was taken hostage – OK? And when my brother and me next come to negotiate, we use the hostage to put pressure on him.'

'My husband doesn't easily give in to pressure.'

'Bully for him. But he might be more inclined to do so, if he thought some harm was going to come to our hostage.'

'I doubt it,' said Mrs Pargeter resolutely.

With a crooked smile, Como drew a pair of wire-cutters out of his pocket. 'I don't think,' he said casually, 'that many men would be that chuffed to take delivery of . . . what shall we say? Something belonging to the hostage. Something very closely attached to the hostage. A little clip of an ear, maybe? Or . . . people very rarely use their little fingers, do they?' Thoughtfully, he opened and closed the wire-cutters. 'I mean, how much do you use your little finger? Maybe for crooking it when you pick up a cup of tea? That's about it, I'd have thought.'

'I may not use it very much,' said Mrs Pargeter, 'but I am very attached to it. And – what is more important – it's very attached to me.'

'I don't think you'd miss it,' said Como. 'And if the loss of your little finger were to help bring ticklish negotiations to a satisfactory conclusion . . . well, you'd be giving it for the greater good, wouldn't you?'

'I think the greater good would be served by all my fingers remaining intact.'

'There we differ.' He was once again opening and closing the wire-cutters in an unnerving way.

'If you're trying to frighten me, Como,' said Mrs Pargeter, sounding calmer than she felt, 'then you're not doing a very good job of it.'

'So, are you criticising me?' His tone had changed suddenly. Now there was paranoia in his voice, paranoia that threatened to break down the restraint with which he held his instinctive violence in check.

He moved to sit beside her on the bed and reached to take her right hand, increasing the pace with which he opened and closed the wire-cutters.

Mrs Pargeter wouldn't have said she was really terrified, but she was nonetheless relieved when the door opened to reveal the tall figure of Damone.

'Stop that, Como!' he said.

Instantly, his brother's fingers stopped their snipping movements as he rose from the bed and backed away.

'Hello, Mr Smith,' said Mrs Pargeter politely. Como giggled again.

Damone dismissed his brother with a jerk of his head towards the door. The code had to be keyed in again to let him out, but though Mrs Pargeter tried to see what his fingers were doing, Como – deliberately, she assumed – kept his sturdy, stocky body between her eyeline and the keypad.

When it was just the two of them in the room, Damone turned on her the full wattage of his smile. 'I'm so sorry,' he said. 'I apologise for my brother. At times he is not very couth.'

NINE

The task of finding Tumblers Tate, as demanded by Mr Pargeter, did not give Truffler Mason and Hedgeclipper Clinton too much of a problem. In fact, their quarry walked, of his own volition, into the crowded No Greens Café the following morning and ordered a Full English Breakfast (with extra Grease).

His demeanour was not that of someone owning up to a crime and handing himself in. If anything, his manner would be best defined as cocky.

Hedgeclipper didn't intend to say anything that might alert their guest to his 'wanted' status and make him do a runner. So, having greeted Tumblers on arrival, he said, 'Come through and have your breakfast in the Function Room. It's warmer in there, and not so noisy.'

To call it a 'Function Room' was perhaps over-generous. It was just a storeroom off the kitchen, but it certainly was quieter. It had the additional advantage that nothing said there could be heard in the main café, and it had two doors that locked. That morning was not the first time the space had been used by Hedgeclipper and Truffler to extract agreements from people who had not initially wished to co-operate.

Issuing instructions to his cook and waitress to keep the breakfast orders (with extra Grease) flowing, the café owner followed Tumblers and Truffler through into the Function Room, locking the door behind him.

Once they were all seated, the suspect on one side of a table facing the other two, Truffler Mason cut straight to the chase. 'Tumblers, we're assuming you know that Mrs Pargeter was abducted from the house in Epping night before last?'

'I had heard, yes.' The reply was far too nonchalant for someone about to suffer from the wrath of Mr Pargeter.

'Well,' Truffler went on, 'I'm sure I don't need to tell you who was responsible for installing the security system there.'

'No. I done it.' The words were spoken with pride.

'There was no sign of forced entry at the house.'

'There wouldn't be. When it's me what's done the security system, nobody can break in.'

'Which means,' Truffler pressed his point, 'that the only way anyone could have got in would be through the front door – right?'

'Right.'

'And the only way anyone could get in by the front door was by using the special codes.'

'I'll buy that.'

'Codes which are only known to Mr Pargeter, Mrs Pargeter . . . and you.'

Tumblers Tate nodded, still showing no signs of discomfort.

'So, the only person who could have given the intruders the relevant codes was you.'

Again, their suspect didn't think that was worth more than a nod.

Hedgeclipper chipped in now, his voice heavy with menace. 'Mr Pargeter particularly dislikes members of his own team doing the dirty on him.'

'I have heard that, yes.'

'And he doesn't like people who do the dirty on him going unpunished. Unfortunately, I don't have my hedgeclipper with me, but –' he drew a long carving knife from a wooden block on the shelf behind him – 'I'm always happy to improvise.'

The café owner moved purposely towards his quarry but was stopped by an upraised hand from Tumblers.

'Before you do something you might regret,' said the locksmith evenly, 'you might be interested to know who I'm working with now.'

'I think we know that,' said Truffler. 'The Batinga Brothers.'

'Ah well, there you are wrong. I don't deny that I did give the Batinga Brothers the codes to the Epping house, for suitable remuneration. But that was just a little freelance job, on the side. I actually have a new main employer.'

'Oh yes?' said Truffler. 'Who's that when he's got his socks on?'

'I am now on the strength of the Lambeth Walkers,' said a triumphant Tumblers Tate.

The words brought his inquisitors to an abrupt halt.

'Ah,' said Truffler, looking to Hedgeclipper for his reaction.

'We'd better check with the boss,' said the café owner. 'I'll phone him.'

He unlocked the door and went through to the café's only phone. The two remaining in the storeroom heard the lock being turned from the outside.

In sepulchral tones, Truffler Mason observed, 'You won't get the same kind of backup with the Lambeth Walkers as you do with Mr Pargeter.'

'I'm not bothered with that,' said Tumblers. 'Always worked on the same principle, I have. Highest bidder. I got a much better deal with the Lambeth Walkers – that's all there is to it. Got very well paid for giving the Epping house codes to the Batinga Brothers, and all.'

A plan was forming in Truffler Mason's mind. 'Since you've now done the job for the Batinga Brothers, you don't owe them any loyalty, do you?'

'No.' With satisfaction, the old man said, 'I don't do loyalty.'

'So, there's nothing to stop you from telling us where the Batinga Brothers have taken Mrs Pargeter, is there?'

'Well, there is, actually, Truffler. What the Batinga Brothers paid me for was not only for giving them the codes but also for keeping schtum about anything else to do with Mrs Pargeter's abduction.' He paused for a moment, before continuing, 'Of course, being, like I said, a "highest bidder" kind of geezer, I might be open to an offer that outbid what the Batinga Brothers paid me . . .'

The bait didn't dangle for long. Mr Pargeter had a rule about never paying money for information . . . at least not until all other possible avenues had been explored. Knowing his employer to be a man of principle, Truffler Mason turned down Tumblers' offer.

At that moment, Hedgeclipper Clinton came back from the main café. The expression on his face and the fact that he didn't lock the door showed the outcome of his telephone conversation. 'You're free to go, Tumblers,' he said, without enthusiasm.

The elderly locksmith rose to his feet. 'I think I'd rather stay,' he said. 'For my Full English (with extra Grease). Get it served through there. And, incidentally, I will not be expecting to receive a bill when I've finished it.'

With some dignity, he went through to the main café.

Truffler looked, without hope, at Hedgeclipper who said, 'Mr Pargeter's not up for challenging the Lambeth Walkers. Not yet. Get the Batinga Brothers sorted, then he'll have a go at his other rivals. Mr Pargeter's never been a man to rush into things. Don't worry. In a few years' time, he'll be the boss of the whole East End. And most of Essex, and all.'

'I know he will,' said a reassured Hedgeclipper Clinton.

Damone had dismissed his brother Como (presumably off to learn how to become more couth – or perhaps less uncouth) and announced his intentions to join Mrs Pargeter for her late lunch. He had confirmed that the time on her watch did mean afternoon rather than the small hours.

She hadn't objected to his proposal. Though he wasn't exactly her ideal lunching companion, Damone Smith (as she, of course, thought of him) was a potential source of information. Though still feeling pretty woozy, she was confident that her feminine wiles might be able to elicit something from him over lunch. Like, for example, where in the world she had been abducted *to*. That'd be a start.

What she did object to, though, was Damone Smith's choice of wine. He produced it from behind his back, as though revealing some special treat. 'When I saw you in Triggers,' he said, 'it was clear that you liked red wine better than white, so, by the same token, I have bought *this* for you.'

And he held out to Mrs Pargeter a bottle of Hirondelle, a

species of fermented grape juice which her husband had told her, on their first date, to avoid like the plague.

'It's rubbish,' he had said. 'Manufacturers don't even tell you what vineyard it's from. Which is a bad sign. And they run this ad campaign . . . pictures of unlikely objects like a mermaid on the slab of a fishmongers with the strapline, "It's about as likely as a duff bottle of Hirondelle". Which is a bit rich, given the fact that every bottle's duff. Total cat's piss.'

He had stopped himself. 'I'm so sorry. I did not intend to use bad language.'

'Don't worry about it, Lionel. I've heard worse.' And she radiated a beam that seemed to envelop him like an electric duvet.

'If we go on seeing each other, Melita, I will never offer you Hirondelle, red or white. That is a solemn promise.'

She didn't know back then quite how solemn Mr Pargeter's promises could be, but she was still impressed. Given this backstory, the bottle proudly presented by Damone really got their lunch off to a bad start. The atmosphere was not improved by their tomato soup, roast chicken and sherry trifle all being delivered at the same time by a sullen functionary with a broken nose. The food, incidentally, had no pretensions to gastronomic status. It was of the kind served up in any number of eateries that didn't really aspire to the name of 'restaurant'.

The quality of the food was the kind of detail that Mrs Pargeter salted away. Her surroundings offered so little information that she seized on any anomaly, anything that struck an odd chord. She was hungry for the smallest detail that might give her a clue to where the hell she was.

That lunch à deux was never going to be a dream date. Damone claimed he wanted to know everything about her, and Mrs Pargeter was determined not to give him any such information. She, on the other hand, only wanted to know where she was being held, along with her chances of getting out of the place, and those were the two things he had no wish to talk about.

What he did want to talk about ultimately, however, was himself. All of his achievements. Which, as far as Mrs Pargeter could tell, didn't amount to very much. This may have been because most of Damone's boasts were prefaced by lines like: 'Well, obviously I can't tell you the full details, but, by the same token, you would be very impressed if I could.'

He also told her about his ambitions. How he planned to make a lot of money, so much that he could pay for all the protection he ever needed in life. How he intended to become a major player in the financial world of the City of London. How he hoped to end up as the master of one of the City livery companies. In a word, by the same token (he kept using that expression, which quickly became annoying), how he proposed to take over the world.

This was all familiar to her. The self-aggrandising male ego. Before she found safe harbour with Mr Pargeter, she had done her fair share of round-the-bay trips on the rough seas of dating. Someone with her looks was bound to have done. And, though she was by nature tolerant and generous, the experience hadn't raised her estimation of men as a gender.

To 'impress' was their dominant motivation. They were all out to impress her. Be it by telling her of their professional success, their sporting triumphs or simply the size of their wallets, this litany of achievement was meant to disarm any opposition and make her desperate to go to bed with them. It wasn't an approach calculated to pay off with her.

One of the factors which attracted her when she first met Mr Pargeter was that he proved so unwilling to talk about himself in any detail. He told her very little about his background and absolutely nothing about his work. He seemed only to be interested in her.

So, her captor's protestations of his own superiority to everyone else fell on deaf ears. She cut through them incisively. 'Damone, can you tell me why I'm here?'

'Obviously –' he produced a leer, intended to be charming but falling far short of the mark – 'it's so that I can enjoy the inestimable pleasure of having lunch with you.'

'Cut the crap!' said Mrs Pargeter. 'Tell me why I'm really here.'

'Well . . . you may have deduced that your husband and I do not see eye to eye on everything . . .?'

'I got that impression when we met at Triggers.'

'Exactly. The dispute concerns a certain area on the edge of the East End reaching into the County of Essex. We both—'

'I know nothing about my husband's work,' she asserted, 'so there's no point in talking to me about the details.'

'How very convenient,' said Damone.

'He's always believed in keeping his work and his home life strictly separate.'

'For good reason.'

Mrs Pargeter thought the remark odd but didn't pick up on it.

'Anyway,' her captor went on, 'in our current negotiations, your husband is proving rather hard to convince that my views on the matter are the correct ones.'

'I'm sure he knows what he's doing,' said Mrs Pargeter serenely.

'Well, by the same token, that's just it, Melita.'

'How did you find out my name?' she demanded, violet eyes blazing.

'I have research resources.'

'Don't use it again. I am very picky about who I allow to use my first name. So is my husband,' she added darkly.

Damone protested, 'I can't call you "Mrs Pargeter" all the time.'

'That's exactly what you can do.'

He looked deflated by this small defeat, but the mood didn't last. 'Anyway, I thought, if you and your husband were separated, *Mrs Pargeter* –' he overloaded the name with sarcasm – 'he might, with a view to your being restored to him, by the same token, be more ready to recognise the strength of my arguments.'

'Arguments over the area of land between the East End and the County of Essex?'

'Exactly so, Mrs Pargeter.'

'So, you're holding me with a view to my husband changing his mind?'

'Again, exactly so.'

'It won't work.'

'Oh, by the same token, I think it will.'

'Once my husband makes a decision, he doesn't change his mind.'

'But don't you think he might be induced to, simply to be reunited with the woman he loves?'

'No.' Mrs Pargeter could be unsentimental when she needed to be. And she somehow knew her husband could, too.

Damone was silent for a moment. He took a sip of his Hirondelle. She hadn't touched hers. Then he spoke. 'I couldn't help noticing, when I came in here, that my brother Como was showing you his wire-cutters . . .'

Mrs Pargeter said nothing.

'My brother is . . . how shall I put this? He has mental problems. "A natural propensity towards violence", I think that's how one of the many psychiatrists he's encountered put it. By the same token, he has instincts which he finds difficult to control. So, if Como were alone in a room with you . . . say this room . . . and he heard that your husband might not be being as co-operative with us as we had hoped . . . it's quite possible that he might feel the urge to snip off one of your fingers . . . only a little one . . . and then send it to your husband . . . as a means of persuading him to see things our way.'

'It wouldn't work,' she persisted.

'Are you suggesting that your husband does not care about you sufficiently to prevent any part of your delightful body being maimed?'

'No, I am not suggesting that.'

'Then what are you suggesting, Mrs Pargeter?'

'I'm suggesting that, before any maiming has taken place, my husband will have arrived here to rescue me.' She spoke with defiance (which she actually felt) and confidence (which was a bit shakier).

Damone let out a dry laugh. 'Oh, I think you are overestimating your husband's abilities, Mrs Pargeter.'

Again, she said nothing.

'However . . .' her captor resumed, 'by the same token, I can reassure you that you are in no immediate danger of being maimed. You see, as it turns out, your husband is not the only one who would hate to see any injury done to that wonderful body.'

'Oh?' Mrs Pargeter wasn't quite sure where this was going.

Damone's tone changed, shifting towards something almost like anguish. 'Mrs Pargeter, since I first heard of your existence, I have longed to meet you. And, even before I met you, I already felt jealous of your husband. Mr Pargeter always contrives to get the best of everything, and I couldn't imagine that that faculty would let him down in choosing a wife. So, by the same token, you have been part of my dreams for a long time.

'And then, when I finally met you at Triggers . . . well . . . my whole universe has been turned upside down. I haven't been able to sleep since that evening. I have dumped all my mistresses. You are the only woman I can think about. You fill my thoughts.

'And the only thing that can restore my sanity, that can make me the happiest man on earth, is for you to leave Mr Pargeter and move in with me.'

Oh God, thought Mrs Pargeter. It's bad enough having a major crook kidnap you. But for him also to fall in love with you . . . that really is the pits.

TEN

Though he didn't want his wife troubled by details of his working life, Mr Pargeter was a stickler for record-keeping. From the moment he transformed from being a sole operator to employing staff, he ensured that all of his company's activities were duly chronicled.

The surname of the person entrusted with this task was Jarvis. No one had ever found out the first name he'd been given at birth, everyone called him 'Jukebox' Jarvis. This was because – as it was explained to those of slower perception who didn't get it straight away – he 'kept the records'.

Though paid handsomely to be his archivist, Jukebox Jarvis did not confine himself to cataloguing Mr Pargeter's doings. He also meticulously recorded the activities of other businesses in the same area of expertise. So, he had built up a comprehensive dossier of all such activities in the East End stretching well into Essex.

It was therefore a no-brainer that Truffler and Hedgeclipper, in their search for their boss's abducted wife, should pick Jukebox Jarvis's brains for any information he might have about the Batinga Brothers.

The Keeper of the Records operated from his front room, which was hemmed in by shelves, all overloaded with dusty cardboard boxes. Inside the boxes were endless much-fingered file cards, scribbled over with Jukebox Jarvis's spidery handwriting in various colours of biro. The different colours denoted the times of updating, according to some chronological system understood only by their creator.

Jukebox was the key to it all. No one else could ever have tracked down an important gobbet of information through the agglomeration of file cards (though apparently his little daughter Erin showed some aptitude for negotiating the labyrinth). But the archivist had only to be given the name of a job or an operative to find the relevant card within seconds. His habit of not always closing the boxes and returning them to their appropriate shelves meant that his workplace always looked as though it had just been visited by a hurricane.

When Truffler and Hedgeclipper were admitted there, they saw something new amid the chaos. In pride of place on Jukebox's desk, with all paperwork and other detritus swept onto the floor, stood a very small television with what looked like a sawn-off typewriter keyboard in front of it. To the right of the keys was what looked like a cassette player. On the screen green writing flickered.

'What the hell,' asked Truffler, 'is that?'

Jukebox Jarvis smiled complacently. 'That, me old mate, is the future.'

'Is it one of them new-fangled word processors?' suggested Hedgeclipper.

'Well, yes it is. But it's so much more than that.'

'How'dja mean?'

'What you are looking at, Hedgeclipper and Truffler, is the Amstrad CPC four six four.'

'Oh,' said Truffler, to whom the name meant nothing.

Hedgeclipper asked, 'So what can this little gizmo –' he gestured towards the keyboard and screen – 'do for you then?'

'What can't it do?' Jukebox gestured to the sagging shelves around him. 'In time, I'll get all this data saved on to it. Like I say, that's the future. Computers are going to take all the drudgery out of human life. This one's only got sixty-four kilobytes of memory, but in the future they'll develop models that can—'

Truffler Mason interrupted. He had more urgent priorities than the golden future of computers. 'Listen, Jukebox, Mrs Pargeter's been kidnapped.'

That stopped him in his tracks. 'Who by?'

'The Batinga Brothers.'

Their name produced the same reaction in him as it did in

everyone else in their world. 'Blimey O'Reilly! They're a nasty bunch for her to get involved in.'

'We know they are, Jukebox. That's why we're here,' said Truffler intensely. 'Dig out anything you've got on the Batinga Brothers! We need to find out where they're holding Mrs Pargeter!'

She had never been prone to crying. Even as a child, when she scraped her knee, she tended to grin and bear it.

She knew a lot of her gender resorted easily to tears. Even used them as very effective bargaining counters. But that wasn't Mrs Pargeter's way. She sometimes wondered what there was in the world which might drive her to tears. If her husband died . . .? But she didn't like to envisage such scenarios.

Her natural mood setting was optimistic. Something would always turn up.

The trouble was, at that moment, none of the things that were turning up were very encouraging.

At the end of their lunch, she had managed to shake off the amorous Damone by pleading a bad headache as a result of the sedative with which she had been immobilised during her abduction. She wasn't making that up. She did feel pretty rotten. And she hadn't been too impressed by Damone's expressions of sympathy . . . particularly given the fact that it was on his orders she'd been anaesthetised.

She did, however, welcome the solitude after her unwanted companion had left, taking the remains of the Hirondelle, of which she had not touched a drop, and not omitting to lock the door behind him. Covertly, she watched his fingers search out the relevant numbers to put into the keypad. But the action was so quick, she couldn't take in more than the first two digits. Still, if she watched every time one or other of the Smith Brothers left the room . . . she might, in time, get all the numbers.

She thought she probably would go back to sleep. But, first, she assessed her situation, wondering if she could tease out, from anything Damone had said, where she was being held and what plans the brothers might have for her future.

The analysis wasn't very constructive. Damone's boastfulness had been frustrating. He had hinted at all kinds of major achievements, without providing any context or detail. In his litany of personal glorification, he had not mentioned a single place name. So, not a single clue to where she was being held.

Because she'd been unconscious when she was transported there from Epping, she had no estimation of how long the journey had taken, so that was no help in orienting herself. And the windowless, unadorned room was equally ungenerous with information.

The only detail that gave her some slight chink of intuition came from the lunch. The way it had been served, all three courses at the same time, along with the style of crockery and cutlery, gave the feeling of a meal prepared in a café. Certainly not home-cooked. So, maybe, it was possible that she was incarcerated near some venue which sold food.

It was a tiny – and possibly not a very reliable – deduction, but it was sufficient to give a lift to someone of Mrs Pargeter's sanguine personality.

She still knew she was in a fix, though. She was the prisoner of two pathologically violent brothers, one of whom wanted to maim her and the other, it seemed, to marry her.

Mrs Pargeter didn't let such thoughts hang too heavy with her. She lay back down on the bed and was soon once again sleeping the deep sleep of the innocent.

'The Batinga Brothers,' said Jukebox Jarvis, 'have always been bad news. You've heard the expression "honour among thieves"?'

Truffler and Hedgeclipper both nodded.

'Well, it applies in a lot of related trades as well.'

Two more nods.

'Not with the Batinga Brothers it doesn't. They have no concept of decency or loyalty. They are very dangerous.'

'Tell us something that's new,' said Truffler impatiently. 'We know how dangerous they are. That's why we're so desperate to get Mrs P out of their clutches.'

'Yeah, come on, Jukebox,' said Hedgeclipper. 'Have you got anything on them?'

''Course I have.' The archivist rose from behind his desk. Unerringly, he went straight to the relevant shelf and pulled out the relevant box. He sat back down again and started riffling through the contents. File cards scattered to either side until he found the ones he wanted.

'OK, how far back do you want to go?'

'How far back can you go?'

'Birth.' Jukebox Jarvis picked up a card and read. 'The Batinga Brothers are two years apart in age. Damone is thirty-four, Como thirty-two. They were born in Dalston to parents who had never broken the law in their lives. The boys were educated at a primary school in—'

'Yeah, we don't need the whole life story,' Truffler Mason interrupted. 'Get on to when they turned criminal.'

'That was at primary school, as it turns out, they—'

'Cut to the more serious stuff,' said Hedgeclipper.

'You don't call burning a primary school down serious?'

'All right,' said Truffler, 'take your point. But we need to know about them when they became a gang.'

'That started at primary school, as well,' asserted Jukebox.

'OK, but once they were up and running . . . how did they operate then? Most important, where do they operate *from*?'

'You mean, have they got an HQ?'

'That's exactly what I mean, Jukebox.'

'You should have said.' The archivist flicked through a stack of cards, ready, as ever, to produce the required data instantly. But his progress slowed. He fiddled back and forth through the cards and clearly couldn't find what he was looking for. 'Well, I'll be . . .'

'What is it?'

Jukebox Jarvis looked up at Truffler Mason, shaking his head in bewilderment. 'The one detail I don't have here is where the Batinga Brothers run their empire from.'

'No clues?'

'Nothing.' He looked disparagingly at the cards which had so let him down. 'Sweet FA.'

'But surely other gangs must have come after them over the years?' Hedgeclipper Clinton suggested. 'Tried to break into their gaff? Haven't there been any shoot-outs?'

'Yeah, plenty. But never on the Batingas' home turf. They tend to do their shooting in restaurants.'

'I think that's appalling,' said Hedgeclipper piously. 'Allowing a place dedicated to serving food to be used as a venue for criminals.' There was an element of 'pot and kettle' in this statement, given the things that had gone on in the No Greens Café Function Room.

'But you'd have thought they'd have somewhere permanent,' said Truffler. 'You know, a place to keep their armoury, that kind of stuff. A place for their Albanian and Romanian heavies to hang out.'

'No evidence of that,' said Jukebox glumly, downcast by his filing system failing him.

Truffler had another thought. 'Have you got lists of the Batingas' personnel, you know, geezers they worked with?'

'Of course I have.' That the question had to be asked was an affront to the archivist's professionalism.

'Well, I was thinking, Jukebox . . . if there's anyone connected with the building trade in there, might be worth following up on them.'

Hedgeclipper caught on quickly. 'I get it. If the Batingas ever needed somewhere permanent . . .'

'Right. Somewhere to lock up some villain from a rival gang . . . or, come to that, a kidnap victim . . .?'

While Truffler spoke, Jukebox was riffling through his data. He quickly found what he was after. It wasn't actually on a card. Two typewritten pages stapled together. He handed them across. 'List of all those who've worked for the Batingas. Updated last Friday.'

Truffler scanned the sheets. He looked to the end. 'I see Tumblers Tate gets in.'

'Yeah, I must change that,' Jukebox reminded himself. 'He's with the Lambeth Walkers now, isn't he?'

'That's right. Oh, and you've put in what jobs all the individual staff done, too. Very helpful.'

Hedgeclipper Clinton was curious. 'What do the black crosses mean?'

'Those are geezers whose contracts have been terminated by order of the Almighty.'

'Oh, I get you. Killed in the line of duty, while doing jobs for the Batingas?'

'That's it, Hedgeclipper.'

'And the red crosses?'

'Those are geezers whose contracts have been terminated by order of the Batinga Brothers.'

'Ouch,' said the café owner. 'Quite a lot of them. The Batingas have a high turnover of staff.'

'They certainly do,' Truffler agreed. 'Makes me even more grateful that we work for a boss who cares about his staff, like Mr Pargeter.'

'Yeah, we're lucky all right.'

Truffler's eye had caught something on the printed sheet. 'Here we are. This guy's got "builder" next to his name. And no crosses. So, he's still around. Yippee!' He could make even that word sound funereal.

'What's the name?' asked Jukebox.

'"Donkey",'

'Just "Donkey"?'

'That's right.'

'Do any of us know someone in the business called Donkey?'

All three of them had to admit that they didn't.

Mrs Pargeter's innocent dreams were interrupted by the reappearance in her prison of Como. He closed the door behind him and locked it, again blocking her eyeline to the keypad. From his trouser pocket, he took out his wire-cutters.

She had no chance to come slowly back to her senses. She was instantly awake.

'I hope you enjoyed your lunch with my brother, Mrs Pargeter.'

'I've experienced better social events.'

'You say that now.'

'I'm not in the habit of changing my mind,' she said with some hauteur.

'You will. When Damone wants something, he is very persistent. And he wants you.'

'Well, I don't want him.'

Como chuckled. 'Damone will win,' he said. 'Having grown up with him, that's one thing I know for certain. Damone always wins.'

Mrs Pargeter didn't grace this assertion with a response. But she was absolutely certain in her own mind that Damone's sequence of successes was about to be broken.

'It is unfortunate,' said Como, 'that your husband is not being as co-operative as we had hoped he would be.'

'That does not surprise me. My husband does not do deals with criminals.'

'Oh, I think you'll find he has done in the past. On many occasions.'

Again, no point in reacting.

'In fact, your husband says we are lying. That we do not have you as our prisoner. So . . .' Como looked down at the wire-cutters and flexed them a couple of times. 'So . . . I'm going to send him something which will leave him in no doubt.'

Mrs Pargeter swung round, so that she was sitting on the side of the bed. She had no expectation that she could overcome her adversary in a fight, but she felt more secure with her feet on the ground.

To her considerable disquiet, Como came and sat beside her.

'So . . . what should I send to convince him?'

She did not resist as he picked up her hand. 'Such a nice little hand,' he said. 'But everyone is so boring about hands. They want them all to be the same. Whereas I think being different is so much more interesting. Anne Boleyn, you know, had six fingers on one hand.'

'That is not true,' said Mrs Pargeter, her voice steadier than her feelings. 'It was a false rumour put around by her enemies to brand her as a witch.'

Como was momentarily taken aback. 'Oh. Well, never mind,' he said. 'I think a hand with four fingers could be almost as beautiful as one with five.'

His hand tightened on her wrist. Mrs Pargeter steeled herself.

She had resolutely not cried when she'd scraped her knee as a child. Surely she could grin and bear the loss of a little finger with equal stoicism?

It felt like a long moment. Then, with a sudden movement, Como grabbed hold of the bottom of Mrs Pargeter's dress and snipped off a six-inch strip of the Laura Ashley fabric of white flowers on a green background.

'This will prove we've got you,' said Como triumphantly, as he moved towards the door. 'If your husband doesn't see sense this time, next it'll be a finger.'

Jukebox Jarvis, Truffler Mason and Hedgeclipper Clinton were still puzzling over the identity of Donkey, the builder who had done work for the Batinga Brothers, when Jukebox Jarvis's office door opened to admit a bright-eyed, dark-haired girl of about ten. 'Hi, Dad,' she said.

'My daughter Erin,' he said, with enormous pride. There was no thought of telling her off for coming in while he was working. Erin could clearly visit her father's office whenever she wanted to.

Appropriate introductions were made and then the girl turned a beady eye on her father. 'What's up?'

'What do you mean?'

'I know that face, Dad. It means you're stuck.'

'Stuck?'

'Yes. There's a piece of information you want to find and you can't find it. And that's why your face has gone all gringey.'

'OK. You may be right,' her father reluctantly admitted.

'Of course I'm right.' Erin perched on the side of his desk and turned a look of great sympathy on him. 'Is it something I can help you with, Dad?'

'Well . . . maybe. All right.'

The two visitors were astonished by how readily the offer of help had been made and the seriousness with which it had been accepted. Erin Jarvis was clearly brighter than the average ten-year-old.

'Tell me what the problem is, Dad,' she said, her manner that of an adult psychotherapist.

'Well, Erin, there's this bloke we want to track down who used to work for . . . for some people we're interested in . . . but all we've got is a name.'

'Hardly even that,' said Hedgeclipper.

'More of a nickname, really,' said Truffler.

'And is this person,' asked Erin, using unexpected language for a ten-year-old, 'of the criminal fraternity?'

'He is, yes,' her father confirmed.

'And what is the name you've got?' Her assurance was amazing. She was effectively chairing a meeting with three grown men.

'Donkey,' said her father.

'I see what you mean about a nickname. Only very vindictive parents would christen a child with that.' Once again, her vocabulary was a source of amazement.

'Right,' she continued in a businesslike manner, 'nicknames. Do you mind if I use the Amstrad, Dad?'

'Be my guest.' Jukebox Jarvis shifted his chair aside so that his daughter could access the keyboard.

'I've been building up a database,' said Erin, as her fingers flicked over the keys, 'on nicknames in the criminal fraternity. Most of them are pretty obvious. They might refer to the kind of work the owner specialises in . . .'

'I see,' said Truffler.

'Or the kind of weapon an individual favours . . .'

'I see,' said Hedgeclipper.

'Or, more often, the nickname can be a corruption of their original name. Smiffy, Bazza, Tel . . . things like that. Then a lot are based on the owner's physical characteristics. Lofty, Shorty, Four-Eyes . . . you know about them.'

All three men nodded agreement. They had worked with many colleagues whose names fitted all of Erin's categories.

The document she had been looking for appeared on the screen. 'I suppose it could be a physical thing with Donkey. He looks like a donkey, perhaps? But I'm not convinced by that. No, I think the "Donkey" we're after is one of those word association scenarios.'

'Er?' said Jukebox.

'Erm?' said Truffler.

'What?' said Hedgeclipper.

By now, Erin had transformed from a CEO chairing a board meeting to an academic giving a lecture to particularly thick students. 'The nickname in that instance derives from a relationship with the surname. Millers were always covered with flour, so a person whose surname was Miller would get called Dusty. The same idea works with Bunny Warren. Or Magna Carter.' She giggled. 'No, actually, I made that one up.

'And, also, given that Donkey is not a very nice thing to be called, we must bear in mind the possibility that the person to whom it was assigned might have changed it as soon as he had some say in the matter.'

Her audience stared at her in amazement.

'So, all we have to do,' she went on, 'is find a surname that would fit with Donkey to make a well-known phrase or saying. Got that?'

The three men looked uncertain.

'For example,' she explained kindly, 'if the surname was Derby, the person could be called Donkey Derby.'

'Oh, I get it,' said Truffler. 'Like Donkey Work.'

'Fine,' said Erin. 'Or it would be if Work was a surname.'

'Donkey's Years . . .?' Hedgeclipper offered.

'Same problem. Do you know anyone whose surname is Syears?'

The café owner had to admit that he didn't.

'Donkey Sanctuary . . .?' said Truffler hopefully.

Erin's little mouth made a moue of disagreement. 'Unusual surname.'

'Donkey Ride . . .?' Jukebox proposed.

'Yes, that'd work, Dad. Do any of you know any crooks with building skills whose surname is Ride?'

Three heads were shaken.

'What about . . .' said Erin, 'Donkey Jacket? Do any of you know any crooks with building skills whose surname is Jacket?'

The three men looked at each other with growing delight before, all together, they pronounced the one word: 'Concrete!'

ELEVEN

Tammy Warnock, the fiancée of the aforementioned Concrete Jacket, was a long-suffering woman. The number of times her wedding had been delayed, owing to the unforeseen absence of her husband-to-be, was approaching double figures. Since Concrete tended frequently to be 'between addresses', the time when he was a free man was mostly spent at Tammy's parents' house.

For an ardent young couple planning a life together, this was not an ideal starting point. The house was a three-bedroomed semi in Harold Wood. Its walls were paper-thin and, since Mr and Mrs Warnock were by nature curious – not to say nosey – the atmosphere was not conducive to the blossoming of young love. Also, because the parents adhered to some arcane religious beliefs, their daughter and her fiancé had to sleep in separate rooms. Any physical contact for them had to go back a generation to the opportunities offered by the backs of cars or cinemas.

So, it was to Harold Wood that Truffler Mason and Hedgeclipper Clinton went directly from their visit to the Jarvises, Senior and Junior.

They were aware of the oppressive atmosphere as soon as they were ushered into the tiny front room. There was a serving hatch through to the kitchen, where Mr and Mrs Warnock were pretending to be busy but clearly bent on hearing anything that was said by their daughter and her fiancé's guests.

Truffler and Hedgeclipper, of course, knew Concrete Jacket, but they hadn't met Tammy before. The first thing they noticed about her was that she was strikingly pretty. The second – and possibly more dominant – impression was that she had a very idiosyncratic style of dress.

As his own appearance – shapeless sports jacket and worn

cavalry twill trousers – indicated, Truffler Mason didn't think much about clothes. Hedgeclipper Clinton was more conscious of the options available and aspired to a sharper – not to say spivvy – style. But both of them were aware of the old belief that certain garments went with certain other garments.

This was clearly not a view to which Tammy Warnock subscribed. Her sartorial instinct seemed to be based on the exact opposite precept, carefully avoiding any two articles of clothing that might be thought to go together.

Above the waist, she was wearing a gold lamé boob tube under a shiny shell suit top in shocking pink and electric blue. Orange hotpants with a big brass buckle were tight over silver fishnet tights, covered lower down by neon yellow legwarmers. The splendid legs ended in fondant green stiletto heels. On her left hand, Tammy wore a single black lace glove, fingerless so that she could show off her proudly worn – and long worn – engagement ring.

Her lovely face could have been an artist's playground for pruned eyebrows, cheekbones contoured by blush and bronzer, frosted lips, blue mascara and more colours of eyeliner than in the entire Dulux range (including the ones that have to be specially mixed for you).

The whole ensemble was crowned with hair in a pink pixie cut that hadn't existed before punk rock was born.

In spite – or perhaps because – of all this, Tammy Warnock looked absolutely stunning. And the expression on Concrete Jacket's face when he proudly looked at her was one of sheer adoration.

But the Warnocks' front room, with the two parents earwigging from the kitchen, was not an ideal venue for the kind of conversation the two visitors needed to have with Concrete.

Truffler took the initiative. Before they'd sat down, he said, 'We've come to take you out for a drink, Concrete. To celebrate Hedgeclipper's birthday. And you're welcome to come, and all, Tammy.'

Dubiously, she screwed up her painted face. 'I bet all you'll do is talk about work.'

'That might happen a bit,' Truffler conceded.

'Then I think I'll stay put,' said Tammy decisively. 'Mum and I have got some wedding dress catalogues to look through.'

What a sensible woman, thought Truffler. Her response was straight out of the Mrs Pargeter songbook. No need to trouble her pretty little overpainted head about her fiancé's work issues.

When they were out of the front door with Concrete, Hedgeclipper Clinton said, in a somewhat bewildered fashion, 'It's not my birthday.'

That morning, Damone suggested that he and his prisoner should again have lunch together. She told him in no uncertain terms what she thought of the idea.

'Don't worry, Mrs Pargeter,' he said, apparently unfazed. 'I can wait. By the same token, I have time on my side. I know you will eventually come around to my way of thinking.'

'You have amazing insight, Mr Smith,' she said.

'Oh?' He warmed to the idea of receiving a compliment from her.

'Yes. You must be the only person in the known universe who can tell the exact date when hell is going to freeze over.'

It took him a moment to work out her meaning. When he did, the smile immediately dropped off his face.

'Mr Pargeter will come round to my way of thinking,' he said sourly. 'He'll cede the territory that I'm interested in. I'm going to win.'

'And how will you do that?'

'Persistence, Mrs Pargeter. Dripping water wears away a stone.'

'What a very appropriate expression for you, Mr Smith.'

'How do you mean?'

'From the moment I first met you . . .'

'Yes?'

'I thought you were a bit of a drip.'

Damone was unamused.

Hedgeclipper Clinton and Concrete Jacket had pints of Carling Black Label. Truffler Mason didn't approve of the way lager – what he thought of as 'continental gassy stuff' – was taking over British pubs. He'd ordered a good old-fashioned pint of bitter.

Concrete was a bit apprehensive about the way he'd been summoned from the Warnocks' house. 'What's this about then?' he asked. 'Is Mr Pargeter not pleased with some job I done?'

'No, no,' Truffler reassured him. 'Mr Pargeter's absolutely delighted with what you done. Still talks about that tunnel to the Midland Bank offices in Braintree. Doesn't he, Hedgeclipper?'

'Certainly does. He says you done that as sweet as a nut.'

'Oh, good.' Concrete Jacket was visibly relieved. ''Cause I don't want to lose my job.'

'No danger of that.'

'Working for Mr Pargeter . . . it's not like any set-up I been with before. Looks after his staff, doesn't he? Holidays, sick pay and all. Almost like going straight . . .' Because he had limited experience of that condition, he added, 'I imagine.'

Truffler provided more ego-bolstering. 'Mr P really rates you, Concrete.'

'Glad to hear it. I been so much more settled since I been working for him. Tammy and me have got a new date inked in for the wedding.'

'Congratulations,' said Hedgeclipper dolefully.

'And this time I think, when we get to the day, we're both going to be there in the church.'

'Good stuff!' said Hedgeclipper.

Concrete Jacket grinned for a moment, then his face took on a more sober expression. 'So, if it's not complaints about my work, why do you want to see me?'

'It's not a complaint,' said Truffler, 'just some information about some work you may have done.'

'Oh, yeah?'

'Before Mr Pargeter recruited you, you was, kind of, freelance – that right?'

'Yes. Worked for anyone if the price was right. Not that a lot of the shysters didn't screw me out of the money what they owed me. You wouldn't believe the way some of them behaved when—'

Truffler interrupted. He and Hedgeclipper had heard

Concrete's litany of misfortune many times before. 'We want to know if you've ever done any work for the Batinga Brothers?'

The predictable pallor flooded into Concrete Jacket's face at the mention of their name.

'Well, yes, I have,' he unwillingly admitted.

Truffler and Hedgeclipper exchanged excited looks. Could it be that they were getting somewhere? 'What you done for them?' asked Hedgeclipper urgently.

'Safe room. Usual spec – can be used for imprisonment or protection, according to who they're keeping in there.'

'And where was this? At the Batinga Brothers' HQ?'

Concrete Jacket shook his head. 'That's the thing, you see, Hedgeclipper. Batinga Brothers don't have a permanent HQ.'

'No, we couldn't find one for them,' said Truffler. 'They run their operations from various restaurants, so far as we could work out.'

'That's it, you're right. They move around.'

'Maybe. But you can't make a safe room move around,' Truffler pointed out. 'Can you?'

'No way,' Concrete agreed. But he seemed unwilling to say more.

'So . . .' asked Truffler after a silence that extended longer than it should have done, 'where did you build it? Underneath some restaurant they worked out of?'

Concrete nodded, still with an air of reluctance.

'So, which restaurant was it?' Truffler persisted.

And Concrete Jacket told them.

One of Mr Pargeter's great skills, the one which set him apart from all potential rivals in the same area of endeavour, was the quality of his planning. Though he could react quickly in a crisis, his preferred method when approaching a job was to have taken time to work out every angle, to anticipate and obviate any eventuality that could possibly go wrong.

And, though he was aware of the jeopardy his wife was in, he had no wish to put her at greater risk by sloppy preparation for her rescue. He had duly received the piece of fabric from her Laura Ashley dress and was under no illusions about the violence the Batinga Brothers were capable of. When they threatened a little finger next, the next bargaining chip would be a little finger.

Working out his plan, Mr Pargeter set up meetings with Truffler Mason, Hedgeclipper Clinton and Gary. He also had Concrete Jacket summoned to his presence and questioned him minutely about the building job he had done for the Batingas. Mr Pargeter had a solid understanding of the construction industry and surprised Concrete by the detail with which he made his enquiries.

Truffler and Hedgeclipper were given an extensive shopping list of goods that would be required for the operation. Some of the items specified surprised them, but knowledge of their boss's track record in such matters prevented them from making any comment.

The important detail they had yet to be told was when the operation would take place. They knew they wouldn't hear that announcement until Mr Pargeter was confident that he'd got all his ducks in a row.

They also knew there was a strong possibility that some ducks – and some people, too – might be harmed in the realisation of Mr Pargeter's stratagem.

All four of them – Truffler, Hedgeclipper, Gary and Concrete Jacket – were sitting in the No Greens Café, waiting for the off. All were nervous. They had been offered the cure-all of the All-Day Full English Breakfast but, for once, its extra-greasy excesses had had no takers.

All were feeling the familiar conflict of emotions that always preceded one of Mr Pargeter's operations. Yes, there was tension, fear even. They wouldn't be human if they didn't feel fear. But also – and overriding other emotions – there was excitement. Working for Mr Pargeter was always exciting.

The No Greens Café phone rang. Hedgeclipper Clinton answered it. He listened, then gave a thumbs up to his companions.

The operation had begun.

TWELVE

It was not Mr Pargeter's habit, except in extreme circumstances, to be present at the activation of his plans. This was in no way due to cowardice. He just recognised the danger of being identified at the scene. Ignorance of what was going on was, as he demonstrated in his care for his wife, a form of protection against hasty conclusions being jumped to by people in authority. And the police were regrettably prone to hasty concluding.

Besides, if he knew he'd covered every detail in his planning – which he always had – his presence at the location's operation was superfluous. It might also be interpreted as mistrust of his employees, whom he had trained to a very high level for just such circumstances.

Sometimes, if absolutely necessary, he would spy on what was being done from a rented office block or similar vantage point. More often, he would control events from what he thought of as his own safe room.

It couldn't have been more different than the one created by Concrete Jacket for the Batinga Brothers. Theirs had been deliberately created to be invisible to prying eyes. Mr Pargeter's was, just as deliberately, public. According to the situation, 'safety' means different things to different people.

Mr Pargeter's safe room of choice was the foyer of the Lancaster Hotel, Chigwell. It was an old-fashioned establishment, much in need of refurbishment. From the 1960s onwards, there had been considerable change in the hospitality industry. Such innovations as en suite bathrooms and telephones in every room had been introduced. Décor had shown aspirations beyond cream wallpaper, dusty curtains drained of colour and grubby patterned carpets.

Not in the Lancaster Hotel, Chigwell it hadn't. The place remained resolutely grim and shabby. The public areas were not allowed sufficient light, which was probably a shrewd move, because it meant no one could see the accumulations of cobwebs in the dark corners. On the higher storeys, those who ventured up there would find one bathroom, with its own en suite toilet – for each landing.

One more thing should be said about the Lancaster Hotel, Chigwell. It was host to a strange aroma. Indefinable, but an associate visiting Mr Pargeter there had once said, 'It smells like a corpse has been hidden behind the wainscot for too long.' And once that idea had been planted, it was an image Mr Pargeter found difficult to weed out of his mind.

A few decades earlier, the Lancaster Hotel, Chigwell would have been described as a 'commercial travellers' hotel' and been the setting for many of the commercial travellers' jokes that went the rounds. But, with time, commercial travellers ceased to exist. Or, to be more accurate, they started calling themselves 'sales representatives' and a rich seam of earthy humour was lost forever.

But though its clientele may have changed, the Lancaster Hotel, Chigwell still did good business amongst people who had to travel for their work and sought out budget accommodation. There were guests coming in and out of the foyer all day, mostly trying – usually without success – to get something done by the comatose reception staff.

There was also a row of six telephone booths in the foyer.

Which was ideal for Mr Pargeter's purposes. At any given point, at least one of them would be unoccupied, enabling him to call a prearranged phone at the scene of his operation, to check progress or issue revised instructions.

While he was there, Mr Pargeter did not sit idly in the foyer. He read. Which might have been a surprise to some who knew him, because he did not have a reputation as a great reader.

The significance lay in what he was actually reading. *The Joy of Sex* was described as 'A Gourmet Guide to Love Making'. Written by Dr Alex Comfort, it was a groundbreaking manual and massive bestseller about what could be performed in bed . . . or indeed on the sofa . . . on the floor . . . or pretty much anywhere else a couple chose to perform on.

Mr Pargeter had no need of guidance to improve the sexual pleasure he shared with his wife, but, for him, the importance of *The Joy of Sex* was that it had a very distinctive cover. Nobody walking past someone reading that book in a murky hotel foyer would forget what they had seen. Even the night porters of the Lancaster Hotel, Chigwell – and a lot of Mr Pargeter's operations took place at night – could not be unaware of the figure sitting in the foyer – and occasionally going into one of the phone booths – because of what he was reading.

If interrogated by the police as to the whereabouts of the gentleman in question, no one could forget where they had seen him.

So, regardless of where the operation he was masterminding might be unfolding, Mr Pargeter wasn't there. He had found the perfect alibi. Many witnesses could confirm that, at the time the police were interested in, he was in the foyer of the Lancaster Hotel, Chigwell. Reading *The Joy of Sex*.

And that was where he was when the Rescue Mrs Pargeter Operation began.

Though Truffler Mason was actually in charge, for the start of the job they relied on Concrete Jacket. He, after all, had built the Batinga Brothers's safe room and knew the codes which would allow access to it.

Gary drove them to the location, curbing his natural instinct to put his foot down to the floor. Mr Pargeter had given him precise instructions. While respecting the young man's instinctive ability to drive extremely fast, his employer was tutoring him in the more difficult task of driving slowly. It was counter-intuitive to Gary, and he had to have explained to him in great detail the importance, on certain occasions, of not drawing attention to oneself.

For the same reason, Mr Pargeter had sourced for their exploit a dark blue Ford Cortina, a car so ubiquitous on Britain's roads that nobody would notice it. Truffler Mason sat in the front next to Gary, with Hedgeclipper Clinton and Concrete Jacket in the back.

None of them was armed. Mr Pargeter had strict rules when

it came to guns. Though there were a few situations which absolutely demanded their being carried, his general view was that the production of a firearm in a stand-off only encouraged your opponent to produce his own firearm. With inevitably messy results.

Another hazard was that if, due to some misunderstanding, the police arrived at the scene, they had a nasty habit of arresting people for the mere carrying of a weapon. So, no guns. Mr Pargeter's operatives were trained in the deployment of negotiation and, when that failed, brute strength.

Hedgeclipper Clinton had on this occasion, however, gone against his boss's instructions. Old habits died hard with him, and so, strapped to the calf of his left leg in their custom-made leather holster, were his trusty hedgeclippers. They had extendable handles, and their blades were notched and battered from earlier encounters. The café owner had no intention of using them. And he certainly didn't want Mr Pargeter to know what he was carrying. It was just that, so much were they part of his identity that, when working on an operation, he felt naked without them.

Truffler Mason also felt naked without his customary distressed sports jacket and cavalry twill. But Mr Pargeter had insisted he wore a uniform and there was no way he was going to go against the boss's advice. He felt quite nervous, though, about why he was wearing the uniform. And he'd never been keen on false beards.

The disguise would become relevant later in the operation when he was required to act as someone else. Truffler Mason was resourceful in the face of many challenges, brave if violence was involved, but he only felt secure when he was being Truffler Mason. The skills of impersonation did not come naturally to him. But, if Mr Pargeter demanded something . . . then that demand had to be obeyed without question.

The four of them had been through the plan in exhaustive detail many times, according to their boss's instructions. And also, again according to their boss's instructions, they went through them yet another time in the car.

Concrete Jacket again described the structure of the safe

room he had built for the Batinga Brothers. 'They was very specific in how they wanted it done. The restaurant was closed for a refurb, so no one suspected what else was going on. And it wasn't like the space had to be dug out. There was existing cellars down there, so it was like a conversion job rather than a new build.

'The safe room itself was pretty straightforward – two rooms side by side, actually. So, I blocked off half the cellar area, usual security features, steel shell and what have you. Entrance down steps from the restaurant, hidden behind sets of shelves. That gets you into a kind of lobby area, where they got one-way-mirror view into the safe room. Set up for sound, so's if they're using it for surveillance or torture, they can, you know, see what's going on.

'But the Batinga Brothers ain't daft enough to only have one exit, so, other side of the room they get me to build this narrow passageway, also got a peephole into the room itself and, like, ladders up to what looks like a manhole cover out of sight in the restaurant car park. That's the route they use for the people, you know, coming in or out. And the bodies, come to that.

'There's like, a little bit that lifts up on the manhole cover and under that's a keypad. Feed the right code into that and it's "Open Jessamy!".'

'I think, Concrete,' said Truffler Mason gently, 'it's "Open Sesame!".'

'Whatever,' said the builder, unperturbed.

'And you know the code that opens up the manhole, right?' asked Hedgeclipper.

'Sure do.'

'You don't think the Batinga Brothers might have changed it?' suggested Truffler gloomily.

'No way. I set the codes. It's a tricky procedure. Only reason they might want to change them was if they'd had a successful break-in. And I been keeping my eye on the place and I know for a fact that they hadn't. Tell you, I'm confident those codes won't have changed a single digit since I installed them.'

It seemed like Concrete's confidence had been well-placed. After they'd parked the Cortina where Mr Pargeter had told them to, he easily located the manhole cover and opened the hinged cap to the keypad.

He keyed in the remembered code. The manhole cover opened up as smoothly as the top of a pedal bin.

'This is too bloody easy,' said Hedgeclipper Clinton. 'No challenge.'

'Don't count your chickens,' Truffler reproved him. 'We haven't got Mrs P out yet.'

'No, but it's going to be a doddle,' said Hedgeclipper.

Concrete Jacket knew exactly what he was doing. He focused a torch on the revealed entrance. 'There's lights inside,' he said, 'but we won't put them on until we've got the cover down again. I'll go in first. You pass the goods to me, then you follow me down – OK?'

With surprising ease for someone who was built on the lines of one of his own brick safe rooms, Concrete lowered himself down into the darkness. Truffler and Hedgeclipper, who had taken the items ordered by Mr Pargeter out of the Cortina's boot, passed the boxes through the open manhole into the builder's waiting hands.

Hedgeclipper went next. Then Truffler uncoiled himself down onto the ladder. (Gary had been left in the Cortina. At first, he'd complained about this until Truffler had reassured him the reason was that they'd be needing his speedy getaway skills. The young man had grinned the grin of someone whose talent was being properly recognised.)

Following whispered instructions from Concrete, Truffler pressed a button which closed the manhole cover above his head.

The lights were switched on and they found themselves in a narrow, solidly bricked area, featuring nothing except the laddered steps they had come down and, opposite, a door with a keypad beside it. Above that was the outlet for an extractor fan.

Concrete Jacket strode towards the door. 'The fact that they hadn't changed the code on the manhole cover,' he pronounced with confidence, 'means there's no chance they will have changed this one.'

A few unsuccessful stabbings into the keypad of various number combinations demonstrated how misplaced his confidence had been.

Mrs Pargeter was deeply asleep. She always slept well. Even in times of jeopardy, she reasoned that her situation would not be improved by her being weak from lack of sleep's reassuring benison. Her natural optimism gave her the hope that, when she woke up, things might be better.

In her prison, she had left the bathroom door ajar, with the light on inside, so that she could see her way if she had to get up in the night. Though she very rarely did. Most nights she enjoyed eight hours of blissful unconsciousness. And any dreams she had were benign ones.

But that night a noise woke her. It was a click of the door to the outside being opened. Light from the adjacent room spilled in for a moment over her head on the pillow, before the door was closed. Mrs Pargeter did not react or shift her position. Her eyelids stayed relaxedly closed.

But her ears were working overtime. Assuming that her visitor was one of the Smith Brothers, she reckoned she was hearing the heavier tread of Damone. This was encouraging in one way. He did not represent the immediate threat of violence that came with Como. On the other hand, he did claim to be in love with her. Damone might offer a different, but no less unpleasant, threat to her body than his brother did.

She was aware of the intruder moving to beside the bed, looming over her. He would be able to see her face in the light from the bathroom. She let out a gentle snore, to emphasise the illusion that she was heavily asleep. Willing her body to remain relaxed, she readied herself for action in case of an attack.

Then Damone spoke. Just a murmur. It seemed that he didn't want to wake her. 'God,' he said, his voice tight with emotion, 'you're beautiful.'

Now Mrs Pargeter liked a compliment as much as the next woman, but this one didn't bring the glow that those from her husband did.

And no glow was generated when her visitor continued his murmur. 'And you're going to be mine, all mine.'

There was what felt to her a long moment of stillness. Then Damone moved back towards the door. The slice of light from the bathroom fell right on the keypad beside it.

Mrs Pargeter's eyes opened a fraction. From behind her thick lashes, she saw the buttons that Damone's fingers pressed.

She had always had a good memory for numbers. And she thought, in the future, she might work on developing that skill, obviously so useful when it came to keycodes.

Truffler Mason, still looking incongruous in his assumed uniform, reminded Concrete Jacket, 'You said there was another entrance to this safe room through the restaurant.'

'Yes.' The builder grimaced. 'But there's no way we could get in there unnoticed. Place is booked out most nights, so we couldn't go in the main entrance without being seen by too many people.'

'What about going the back way, through the kitchens? I thought you said that's where the entrance to the cellar is.'

'You're right, Truffler, but the kitchens'll be full, and all. There's a lot of staff to run a place like this. No way they won't notice us going through. And, even if we could get there unnoticed,' said Concrete, adding another dampener to the proceedings, 'we'd hit a problem, anyway.'

'Like what?'

'I co-ordinated the codes for the front and back doors of the safe room, inside and out. They're the same. If we was in the restaurant cellar, facing that keypad, we'd stand no more chance of finding the right code than we do with this one.'

General gloom descended on the three of them.

'Any chance,' hazarded Hedgeclipper, pointing at the wall ahead of them, 'we could smash this down?'

The very suggestion caused deep affront. 'No bloody chance at all! When Concrete Jacket builds a safe room, there's a clue in the name. The "room" is "safe" from any attack. Tell you, Hedgeclipper, what you see in front of you could survive a direct hit from a nuclear bomb.'

'Sorry, Concrete. I didn't mean—'

'Yes, you did. I'll forgive you this time, but if I ever again hear you casting nasturtiums like that . . .'

'You won't, Concrete, you won't!' Hedgeclipper hastened to reassure him.

'What's that up there?' asked Truffler suddenly, pointing at the wall above the door. 'Thing that looks like the outer grille of an extractor fan?'

'It's the outer grille of an extractor fan,' said Concrete Jacket.

'Presumably,' Truffler proceeded, 'attached through the wall to the extractor fan itself?'

Concrete Jacket confirmed that was the case.

'An extractor fan which you installed yourself . . .?'

A nod.

'And would be entirely capable of uninstalling?'

Concrete Jacket nodded once again.

'That won't help,' said Hedgeclipper Clinton, drenched in gloom. 'We're all too big to climb through the aperture.'

'Climbing,' said Truffler Mason, 'is not the only thing you can do through an aperture.'

Mrs Pargeter wasn't woken by the noise. She hadn't gone back to sleep after the unnerving visit of Damone. Having waited some five minutes, repeating the code to herself, she dared to find a scrap of paper and scribble it down. She then concealed the scrap inside her bra.

Actually knowing the code had given her confidence a huge boost. How she would use her new knowledge, when she would time her escape for . . . those were details she'd have to plan for.

And when she heard the scraping sound from the bathroom, her confidence grew into euphoria. It never occurred to her that she might be at risk from whoever was making the noise. She had always known that her husband would sort out her release. It had only been a matter of time.

And now, the rescue operation was under way.

* * *

'You all right up there?' Truffler called from the bottom of the ladder.

''Course I am,' Concrete Jacket replied. 'I put the bloomin' thing in, didn't I? So, I should be able to take it out.' There was a sound of plastic being shifted. 'Bathroom light's on. Suggests there's someone in the place.'

'There certainly is,' said a warm voice from the other side of the wall. She recognised the speaker. 'Good to hear your voice, Concrete. I knew the old man'd get me out of this some way.'

'Well, yes,' the builder called through the hole. 'But we're not quite there yet. We still don't have the code that opens front and back doors on this place.'

'Oh, I do,' said Mrs Pargeter casually. And she spelled out the numbers she had watched Damone key in while he thought she was asleep.

Concrete Jacket repeated the numbers to his companions. 'Key it in, Truffler!' he said. 'See if the door shifts. I got to stay up here to give Mrs Pargeter instructions.'

'Mrs Pargeter? You mean you found her?'

'Certainly have.'

Truffler Mason opened the hinged cover on the keypad and pressed in the numbers. After the last one, he heard a resolute click from the door. He turned the handle. Another click and he could feel no resistance. 'I can open it, Concrete.'

'Wait! Just got to give some instructions. Mrs Pargeter, will you stand back in the doorway to the other room?'

'Of course I will, Concrete,' came the response. 'Right, I'm there.'

'Stand by, Mrs P. I'm coming down, Truffler. I'll do the next bit.' The builder again belied his bulk as he scuttled down the ladder.

He faced the exposed keypad and pressed a small red button beneath it. There was a mechanical grinding sound but, from the perspective of the three men, nothing changed.

On the other side of the wall, however, Mrs Pargeter watched dumbstruck as the tiled wall in front of her split down the middle and drew apart like a pair of curtains. The vanity unit, basin and all, shifted to the left with its half of the wall, to reveal a strong metal door with a keypad beside it.

As she moved forwards, Mrs Pargeter was delighted to see the door open to reveal the welcome outline of Concrete Jacket.

She rushed towards the builder and threw her arms around him. It wasn't a hug of desperation; it was a hug of pure ecstatic glee.

Then, although it was the first time she was meeting them, she gave equally bountiful hugs to Truffler Mason and Hedgeclipper Clinton. Little did she know then what significant roles the two of them would play in her future life.

It was just as well that Gary, frustrated in the Cortina, didn't witness these hugs. They would have fulfilled his every fantasy.

(Although, keeping in mind her generous nature, had he been present at the scene, Mrs Pargeter would definitely have given him a big hug, too.)

THIRTEEN

Mrs Pargeter was surprisingly agile up the stairs to the manhole cover and soon she and Hedgeclipper Clinton were at ground level in the car park.

Down below, there were still tasks for Truffler Mason and Concrete Jacket to perform. The builder helped Truffler carry the boxes from the car into the secret area. From there, following Mr Pargeter's instructions, they took the goods through to the restaurant's cellar.

'Don't know why,' Truffler observed, 'Mr Pargeter didn't want to set off this lot actually in the safe room.'

Concrete Jacket explained, 'That room which, you may recall, I built, is too strong for any explosion to do anything but spoil the décor. It'd contain the bombs, stop their effects spreading, which, you may recall, is exactly what Mr Pargeter doesn't want to happen.'

'Yes, of course, sorry. Should have thought of that,' said Truffler humbly.

Concrete grinned. It was rarely that he could score a point off the more intellectually gifted Truffler Mason. He also felt proud of the impregnable fortress he had built.

After they'd gone back through the safe room to the area with the ladder, Concrete Jacket returned the bathroom to its former state so that, when her captors next visited, there would be no clue as to how Mrs Pargeter had been sprung from her jail. A genuine locked room mystery.

The manhole once again closed, the four of them stood in the evening chill.

'Part one of Rescue Mrs Pargeter Operation completed,' Truffler Mason announced.

'Oh, is there a part two?' she asked.

'Not so much for you,' he replied lugubriously. 'All we need to do with you is get you safely back to Mr P. Rescue Mrs Pargeter Operation Part Two mostly involves me. That's why I'm wearing this bloomin' uniform.'

'So, what does your extra bit involve?'

'Mrs Pargeter, your husband is a very clever man when it comes to planning, and one of the clever things he does is to insist that the fewest number of people possible know details of those plans.'

Mrs Pargeter understood instantly. 'Yes, I've often heard him say that.' She didn't ask any further questions.

'Right,' said Truffler ponderously. 'I'd better get to the restaurant. But I would like to say—'

What he would have liked to say they never knew, because suddenly Como was in the midst of them waving his wire-cutters.

'You won't get away with this!' he cried. In a nanosecond, he was holding Mrs Pargeter in a bearhug, which still enabled him to grasp the blades of his wire-cutters against the little finger of her right hand. 'Come near me and she loses the finger!'

What happened next happened so quickly that none of them could give an accurate account of it afterwards. Hedgeclipper Clinton, who was behind Como, reached into his trousers and extracted the implement which gave him his name.

With one deft movement, he brought the shears down on the psychopath's hand. Mrs Pargeter managed to pull her finger free as the metal blades pulverised the wire-cutters. Como let out a yelp of pain and looked in bewilderment at the ground, which was where his little finger had come to rest.

Concrete Jacket was very efficient in the way he trussed Como up. And gagged him.

'Don't leave him too near the building,' said Truffler. 'We don't want him to get hurt . . . any more than he already is.'

They left the kicking but immobilised body tied to a tree at the edge of the woods.

Mrs Pargeter and Hedgeclipper Clinton got into the Cortina. And Gary's moment arrived. He roared out of the car park as if from the Formula One grid.

Truffler Mason adjusted his uniform as he turned back towards the restaurant, to complete stage two of the Rescue Mrs Pargeter Operation.

As directed by Mr Pargeter, Truffler entered the building through the kitchens. It was there that the risk to staff would be greatest. And there that Mr Pargeter had told him to generate maximum panic.

So, following instructions, Truffler Mason, uniformed and bearded, burst in through the kitchen doors, shouting out, 'I'm from the Gas Board!'

(There'd been discussion as to whether he should say this or 'I'm from British Gas!', following the authority's recent renaming. Mr Pargeter had ruled that idea out firmly, saying, '"Gas Board" is what people remember.')

'And,' Truffler went on, following his script, 'a gas leak in this restaurant has been reported! Evacuate the building instantly!'

The chefs and waiting staff, from long experience of working in kitchens, didn't need a second telling. They all had heard stories of disasters caused by gas leaks. Some burst through the door by which Truffler had entered, others rushed out via the restaurant.

This was good news for the bearded man in the British Gas uniform. The fleeing waiters and waitresses had engendered so much panic amongst the dining clientele that, by the time he went through to shout more warnings, the space was almost empty. 'Get out quickly!' he shouted to the stragglers. 'And keep a good fifty yards from the building! It could go up any minute!'

Within seconds, Truffler Mason was alone in the restaurant. He went to the phone on the reception desk and rang a remembered number. It was answered from a booth in the foyer of the Lancaster Hotel, Chigwell. 'All good,' said Truffler. 'We've got her! And she'll be with you at the hotel in as long as it takes Gary to drive there!'

The recipient of the phone call went back to reading *The Joy of Sex*. But he was too excited to take much of it in.

Truffler Mason replaced the receiver, went back to the kitchen and opened the cellar door. He took a remote control out of his uniform pocket and pointed it towards the goods they had left there. The red light that glowed at the end of the remote was answered by a red light from one of the boxes.

Unhurriedly, he removed his uniform jacket and false beard, then let himself out through the kitchen door. A large crowd of confused staff and diners circled round the front of the building. Obediently, they were at a good fifty yards' distance.

Unnoticed by a crowd too concerned with their own safety, Truffler insinuated himself in behind the restaurant's owner. He checked his watch.

On cue, a huge explosion sounded from the bowels of the building. Within seconds, flames filled the whole interior and were licking hungrily, through the smashed windows, at the edges of the roof.

Truffler Mason treasured the expression he saw on the face of Lennie, as he watched the total destruction of Triggers Restaurant.

Truffler could have told him, though. It was never a good idea to get on the wrong side of Mr Pargeter. And, in the list of such offences, allowing the Batinga Brothers to operate from your premises is about as bad as it can get.

'I'm afraid, Melita,' said Mr Pargeter, 'that is one restaurant we will not be visiting again.'

They were sitting at home with a bottle of champagne in an ice bucket and two full flutes.

'No. Very sad,' his wife agreed. 'I read about it in the local newspaper. Gas leak, they reckoned.'

'Did they? I don't think the police have made a full investigation yet.'

'Police?' Mrs Pargeter echoed. 'Why? Is there a suspicion of something criminal being involved?'

'Who knows?' said her husband. 'I think it's probably the police once again being over-zealous.'

'They're a fine body of men – and women,' said Mrs Pargeter.

'They certainly are,' Mr Pargeter concurred.

'But it's terribly bad luck for Lennie.'

Her husband made no comment. It wasn't the moment to say that that was what happened to people who did the dirty on him.

'I hope,' his wife went on, 'he was properly insured.'

'Melita, my love . . .' Mr Pargeter deftly redirected the conversation. 'I don't want to dwell on the details or revive unhappy memories for you, but while you were imprisoned by them, did either Damone or Como hurt you in any way?'

'I wasn't best pleased by being abducted, if that's what you mean.'

'No, it isn't exactly. Did either of them . . . er, molest you?'

'Oh, I see what you mean. Como did, sort of, well, I suppose he threatened me.'

'With his wire-cutters?'

'Yes.'

'But you weren't hurt?'

'Lost a bit of my Laura Ashley dress. But I think you had that delivered to you.'

'Yes, I did.' There was a silence, then he asked, 'And what about Damone . . .?'

'Molestation? He came on to me a bit. Claimed to be in love with me.'

'Oh yes?' The conversation was clearly a lot more serious for Mr Pargeter than it was for his wife. 'What did he say?'

'Just that . . . it was quite flattering, actually, to both of us. He said you always got the best of everything – and now you'd got the best wife.'

'Did he say he was jealous of me?'

'Not in so many words, he didn't, but that was obviously what he meant.'

Mr Pargeter nodded with satisfaction. 'Good,' he said. 'That means I won again.'

Mrs Pargeter deduced that the rivalry between the two men was long-running and deep. But she didn't enquire any further. It was none of her business. The history of that antagonism was something that fitted very firmly into her husband's 'work' compartment.

Anyway, he seemed reassured by the dialogue they had just shared. 'While I was in Chigwell . . .' he said, changing the direction of the conversation.

'Oh yes?' she said. 'I must say I didn't care for that hotel where Gary drove me to.'

'No, very far from salubrious, I agree. But I don't always get a choice in where I have to do business.'

Mrs Pargeter did not comment. Like her husband, she respected the barrier between his work and what he talked about in their Epping house. 'I did notice, though,' she giggled, 'that someone had left a copy of *The Joy of Sex* in that hotel foyer.'

'Imagine that.' Mr Pargeter joined in the giggle.

'Imagine anyone needing a book to tell them how to do it.' Mrs Pargeter's giggle had become a full-throated laugh.

They held hands and looked at each other across the table with the confidence of two people who did know how to do it. Very well indeed.

'Anyway, Melita my love,' he went on, 'having to spend time in Chigwell, I was looking around there and saw a very nice building plot for sale.'

'And you thought of buying it to build something you need for a work project, did you?' There was something admonitory in her tone. A warning that he might be straying towards conversation about work.

'No, no,' he replied. 'I was thinking of buying it for us. A place where we can build our dream house. It's very secluded, the plot. We wouldn't be overlooked or anything like that.'

'Oh,' said Mrs Pargeter, with a glint of disappointment in her violet eyes. 'But I like the little house we've got here in Epping.'

'I agree. It is delightful. But . . .' Her husband grimaced. 'The fact is, Melita my love, that recent events —' he didn't need to spell it out — she knew what he was referring to — 'have left me less than happy about the security arrangements we have here.'

'Oh?'

'Think about how easily the Batinga Brothers managed to abduct you from here.'

'Sorry, Lionel? Who are the Batinga Brothers?'

'Oh, slip of the tongue. I meant to say "the Smith Brothers".'

'Yes, of course. Easy mistake to make,' said his wife innocently.

'Well, I was just thinking, Melita my love, this house is, as you say, lovely. But, if we were to build somewhere from scratch, design it ourselves . . .'

'What, no architect?'

'If we tell him exactly what we're after, Concrete Jacket'll build it for us.'

'Oh yes. I'm so glad that's a success, him working for your company.'

'All down to you, Melita my love. What a great recruitment expert you've turned out to be.'

She smiled at the compliment. 'If I can help someone with a criminal record to get a legitimate job . . . and if at the same time that person can be useful doing stuff for my husband . . . well, what's not to like in that scenario?' She was, of course, far too discreet to ask what sort of 'stuff' someone like Concrete Jacket might be doing for Mr Pargeter.

'Anyway, a place purpose-built for us, Melita my love . . . how do you like the idea?'

'Perfect. But not now. In the future. A dream for the future, eh?'

'A dream for the future,' Mr Pargeter confirmed.

They clinked champagne flutes and drank.

Of course, the police investigated what had happened at Triggers Restaurant. It didn't take long for their forensic team to prove that a gas leak had nothing to do with the conflagration. It had been triggered by explosives hidden in the basement.

So, they were extremely interested in the true identity of the bogus Gas Board official who had sounded the alarm. But, although he had been seen by so many witnesses, they didn't get anywhere in tracking him down.

In their investigations into the remains of the restaurant, they were also intrigued to find a separate pair of rooms built into the basement area. The trouble they had breaking into this stronghold would have made Concrete Jacket very proud. And when they did finally get inside, the amount of cocaine they found stashed in there was sufficient to ensure that Lennie, the restaurant's owner, got sent down for a very long sentence.

In vain did he protest that he had only allowed the safe room to be constructed in his cellar following threats of violence. Even that early in their professional careers, the Batinga Brothers had developed the habit of employing very expensive lawyers. The two had cast-iron alibis for the night of the unfortunate events at Triggers and no wrongdoing of any kind could be attributed to them.

As for the idea of any inquiries being made into the activities of Mr Pargeter and his associates ... well, it never happened. Though it was established that he and his wife had been frequent diners at the restaurant, that, it was agreed, was their only connection with the place.

Equally, though members of Mr Pargeter's organisation, like, say, Truffler Mason and Hedgeclipper Clinton, might have witnessed actions by the Batinga Brothers which could lead to their arrests, there was no way they were going to share that information with the police. Though both strong supporters of the principle of justice, they weren't about to start an enquiry that might, all too easily, lead to investigations into their own activities. Or, indeed, those of Mr Pargeter himself.

There were two consequences of the events in Theydon Bois, of which the police were completely unaware. The first was that Damone Batinga could not forget what had happened, how he had once again been bested by Mr Pargeter. And how jealous he continued to be of the beautiful wife his rival possessed. Over the years, his infatuation with her did not die, but rather curdled into a deadly obsession. Damone Batinga was unhealthily determined to have Mrs Pargeter as his own. He nursed a fantasy of having her by his side when he took over the mastership of a City livery company.

The other thing that happened was that, in the confusion following the destruction of Triggers Restaurant, the Batinga Brothers rather took their eyes off the ball in relation to the area of East London and Essex about which they were in dispute. This was the 'turf war' that Como Batinga had talked about – indeed the reason why Mrs Pargeter had been abducted, in an attempt to make Mr Pargeter concede.

Well, he didn't concede. In fact, he took over the whole area, using his unique powers of persuasion to encourage any personnel who had sided with the Batinga Brothers to change their allegiance sharpish. No one in the relevant location questioned the fact that Mr Pargeter was now the boss.

But, of course, Mrs Pargeter didn't know anything about any of that.

FOURTEEN

Which was why, thirty years after the events which have just been chronicled, Mrs Pargeter could claim to Truffler Mason and Hedgeclipper Clinton that she'd never heard of the Batinga Brothers. Now, if they'd asked her about the Smith Brothers, that would have been a very different matter.

She held court with them over Dom Perignon in a private room at Greene's Hotel.

'So,' she said again, 'I want you to set up this meeting for me.'

'With the Batinga Brothers?' asked Truffler unwillingly.

'With Damone. He seems to be the brains in the outfit.'

'Remind us,' said Hedgeclipper Clinton, with equal lack of enthusiasm, 'why you want to see him.'

'So that I will have the information to enable me to bring about the collapse of his criminal empire.' She made it sound so easy.

Truffler Mason tried another argument to put her off. 'He's hardly likely to agree to a meeting whose sole purpose is to bring down his criminal empire, is he?'

'No, I agree,' said Mrs Pargeter equably. 'The pretext for the meeting would be that I want to negotiate a deal for Short Head Shimmings.'

Hedgeclipper Clinton let out a sceptical whistle. 'The Batinga Brothers don't negotiate deals.'

'Could you please set up a meeting for me with Damone Batinga?' There was steel in the charm with which the words were spoken.

Truffler and Hedgeclipper knew that time was tight. Short Head Shimmings and his mother Athena were safe in Devon in the care of Holy Smirke, Ernestine and her daughter Mignon, but even HRH's NowhAirBnB arrangements might not be secure for very long against the might of the Batinga Brothers.

They were also unhappy about the idea of setting up the meeting with Damone Batinga which Mrs Pargeter had demanded. Her belief that she had been kidnapped by the Smith Brothers rather than the Batinga Brothers suited them. It meant she didn't feel she was still under threat. But her illusion could not be maintained if Truffler and Hedgeclipper did as she asked and set up the meeting.

They worried about how she would react to being faced by someone responsible for her kidnapping thirty years before. But they again told themselves that, if they didn't oblige, Mrs Pargeter was likely to go elsewhere for help. And they would rather they were in control of the narrative.

Reluctantly, they considered the logistics of the challenge they had been tasked with.

And they knew that, however the job got done, it would mean using more of their contacts from the past.

'Who do we know who's big in the financial world?' asked Truffler.

'Well, there's Charlie Wolfe,' suggested Hedgeclipper.

'Oh, yeah. I remember him,' said Truffler. 'Used to deal with Mr Pargeter's tax affairs.'

'That's the geezer. Real name was "Neville" but answered to "Charlie". Always insisted his "Charlie" was short for "charlatan".' The hotelier chuckled at the recollection.

'Yeah. But now he's gone up in the financial world, he's changed his nickname.'

'What to, Truffler?'

'"Canary" Wolfe.'

The nickname was apposite for the location of the accountant's office in Canary Wharf. As 'Charlatan' Wolfe, he had stepped over the line into criminality in avoiding tax for Mr Pargeter. As 'Canary' Wolfe, he remained just the right side of that same line in organising legal tax-avoidance schemes. Nothing had really changed.

Except, of course, that Neville Wolfe was now respectable,

an esteemed City figure whose name on the headed notepaper of various companies was much sought after and expensively bought. His client list encompassed the great and the good from the worlds of finance, politics, show business and sport. At the parties he gave, he was the only one who nobody recognised. Which was exactly the way he wanted things to stay. He was the originating master of a recently formed City livery company. And his name was even mentioned in discussions about the candidates to be the next Lord Mayor of London. He had all the required qualifications.

The moment Truffler Mason mentioned his connection to the late Mr Pargeter, his call was put straight through to Neville Wolfe. Truffler and Hedgeclipper were invited to come to his Canary Wharf headquarters as soon as possible.

The tax-avoidance expert worked from a corner office on the eighteenth floor of his block. The two glass sides of his office presented extensive views over London. The Thames and the O2 Arena featured strongly in the vista.

But he had not gone so far up in the world as to forget his less elevated beginnings, or to disown his colleagues from those less lavish times. He offered refreshments to Truffler and Hedgeclipper. Soon they were all enjoying a very fine Islay malt from his well-stocked drinks cabinet.

'Oh, I just remember the sheer fun it was working for Mr Pargeter,' he said, brushing a drip from his immaculate Savile Row suit. As he spoke, he visibly relaxed. In sympathy, his vowels relaxed, too, degrading from cut glass to jam jar as his East End roots reasserted themselves.

'Do either of you have any recollection of the Hoxton Hijack?' he went on.

'Do we?' asked Hedgeclipper Clinton, already giggling.

'And how!' Truffler Mason, who wasn't prone to giggling, still managed to crack a smile.

'I remember,' said Canary Wolfe, 'Mr Pargeter generally kept me away from the actual scenes of operations. Going along with his old regular "what you haven't seen you can't answer questions about" principle. But on that occasion, he thought it might be good for me to get an insight into what his organisation actually did. So, I wasn't, like, involved in the job itself. I was tucked away in a greasy spoon what he'd recommended to me. Mr Pargeter had given me a minder – bloke called "Knuckles" Knight – and from there we could see everything that went on.'

'Yeah, it was one of Mr Pargeter's best plans. A classic,' said Hedgeclipper, with recollected relish.

Truffler Mason looked less enthusiastic. 'It was a good *plan* . . .' he said, clearly about to detail some of its faults.

'Only reason you didn't like it, Truffler,' Hedgeclipper chipped in, 'was because it involved you wearing a disguise.'

'All right,' the private investigator grudgingly conceded, 'maybe that had something to do with it.'

'Good disguise, though, it was,' Hedgeclipper reassured him. 'I was wearing it, and all. London Electricity Board workers we was, dealing with an emergency what meant we had to dig up a bit of the road. Hoxton Street it was.'

'Except, of course,' Canary Wolfe pointed out, 'you wasn't digging up anything. Sure, you had one of them stripy tent things on the roadside but there wasn't nothing under it.'

'There was,' Hedgeclipper protested. 'Gary the driver was under it, ready to drive off the lorry after we'd done the hijack.'

'As ever,' said Truffler, now caught up in the fever of recollection, 'Mr Pargeter's research was spot on. Lorry full of pallets with crates of spirits on them. Whisky, gin, vodka, the lot. Going to stock up Tesco branches round the East End. Ready for Christmas.'

'Of course,' said Canary Wolfe, 'timing's perfect. Lorry stops for the London Electricity Board roadworks . . . well, what the driver thinks is the LEB roadworks.'

'And then, I remember,' Hedgeclipper joins in, 'Truffler and me's got the lorry cab doors open, one each side, pulled out the driver and his mate. Before you can say "Reggie Kray", Gary's up in the cab, driving hell for leather over the LEB tent and back to the next port of call.'

'And Knuckles Knight's got a motorbike,' said Canary Wolfe, 'and he drives me, like he's in the Isle of Man TT, to the underground car park where the next bit of the operation takes place. Tesco logos taken off the sides of the lorry and replaced.'

'And that's where Mr P's always so clever,' Truffler remembered fondly. 'He puts Sainsbury's livery on one side of the lorry and Waitrose on the other.'

'Yes, I never understood why he did that,' Canary admitted.

'It's obvious. It's so that, when the lorry's driving through the streets, the witnesses what see it contradict each other. Half of them say it was a Sainsbury's lorry, half say it was Waitrose,' Truffler explained. 'Makes the barristers' jobs dead tricky if the case ever come to court. Though, of course, being a Mr Pargeter operation, the case never would come to court.'

'Oh, gotcha, Truffler.'

The private investigator grinned as he picked up the story. 'Then Gary drives the lorry, all sober and correct, like, to this big lockdown Mr P's got in Chelmsford. And all the pubs in Essex and the East End have very good Christmases, because they all got their spirits at knockdown prices.'

'Genuine Robin Hood, Mr Pargeter was,' Canary mused in admiration. 'Took from the rich and give to the poor.'

'We will not see his like again,' Hedgeclipper Clinton intoned solemnly.

The three men shared a moment of respectful silence.

Then Canary Wolfe said, 'But I dare say it wasn't about the great Mr Pargeter that you come to see me.'

'Well, it's not unconnected,' said Truffler.

And he described the situation in which they found themselves. Or, perhaps, to be more accurate, the situation in which Short Head Shimmings had landed them.

Needless to say, they did not need to fill in the background for Canary Wolfe. He already knew, at least by reputation, most of the characters involved.

When Truffler had finished his narrative, the financier let out a low whistle. 'Half a million owing to the Batinga Brothers . . . I don't think there are many people who have come out of that situation alive.'

'No, there aren't,' Truffler agreed. Then he was guilty of a small lie, using Mrs Pargeter's pretended reason for the meeting.

'Which is why we want to see Damone Batinga, see if we can make some kind of deal with him. To save Short Head Shimmings's life.'

'Not many people who have tried to make a deal with Damone Batinga are still alive,' Canary observed gloomily.

'We've got to try,' Truffler insisted. 'HRH's hideaways are good, but no one stays hidden for long when the Batingas are after them.'

'You're right there.'

'So,' asked Hedgeclipper urgently, 'do you have a line to Damone Batinga?'

'Oh yes,' Canary replied. 'In the City, everyone knows everyone else. I see Damone a lot socially. He's actually a member of my livery company.'

'Thought there'd be some connection like that,' said Truffler. 'So, can you fix up a meet with him?'

'What, for you two?' He sounded dubious.

'No. For Mrs Pargeter.'

'For Mrs Pargeter!' Canary Wolfe echoed in delight. 'I'll get on to it straight away!'

'They do us very well here, don't they?' said Athena Shimmings.

'Yes, yes,' her son agreed.

'Another nice meal.'

She looked down at the remains of their lunch, all of which had been eaten up with great relish. Mignon really was an excellent cook. Their arrangement was that she would send down all three courses, with the wine, in the dumb waiter, then come down in person to serve the first course, leaving the rest of the meal in a superior kind of hostess trolley. At the end of the meal, leaving a suitable interval for them to digest, she would return to load all of the dirty dishes back into the dumb waiter.

The intention of this system was to allow the two Shimmingses, mother and son, to enjoy their meal undisturbed. This, Athena opined, was very thoughtful on the part of their hosts. Short Head Shimmings, on the other hand, would have given anything for some kind of disturbance. Loving his mother did not automatically encompass loving her conversation. There is a finite number of times a person can be told how nice everything is. But, in their NowhAirBnB hideaway, there was nothing to stop Athena Shimmings continuing uninterrupted during waking hours.

Her son's attempts to keep waking hours as short as possible had been unsuccessful. His arguments about the benefits of early nights were frustrated by his mother's habit of suddenly finding a new reserve of garrulousness around ten thirty at night. And his attempts to have lie-ins in the mornings were defeated by heavy bangings on his bedroom door and cries of 'Out of bed, sleepyhead!'.

To add to his woes, Athena Shimmings, deeming the use of either laptop or mobile phone in her presence to be bad manners, had demanded that Mignon should take away both of his devices for safekeeping. For Short Head, who hadn't gone a day without making a bet since early childhood, this was a refined form of torture.

Another reason why he objected to their uninterrupted lunches was down to who might do the potential interrupting. After initial introductions, the prisoners – because, although he knew he was there for his own protection, it still felt like being a prisoner – had not seen anything of Holy Smirke and Ernestine. All their needs had been catered for by Mignon. And, as the days went by, increasingly Short Head Shimmings thought about another of his needs he wouldn't mind her catering for.

He dared to conjecture that Mignon was not uninterested in him, either. Maybe the attraction came from the shared experience of dealing with dominant mothers, but both were soon, at meal delivery and dirty dish collection times, exchanging little intimate smiles which had effects on them not achievable by any old smiles.

So, as he sat over the empty lunch dishes that day, Short Head Shimmings had reasons to feel discomfort. The truth that should have disturbed him most – the fact that the Batinga Brothers were after his blood – featured relatively low on his list of irritants. The fact that he couldn't make a bet on anything – he was by then prepared to take a punt on how long a passing ship took to go from one side of their picture window to the other – was a continuing anguish. The impossibility of spending time alone with Mignon merely rubbed salt into his other wounds.

And, more annoying even than those tortures, there was the fact that he had to listen to his mother's conversation.

'Another nice meal,' Athena Shimmings repeated. A silence. 'Come on, Cecil, don't you agree?'

That was the real pain about dialogue with his mother. No remark by her was allowed to stand on its own. Every statement demanded a reaction from him.

He dutiful supplied one. 'Yes, very nice,' he said.

He looked at the dishes. That day, Mignon had supplied them with Tourin à l'Ail, a garlic soup, Magret de Canard with Pommes de Terre Dauphinoises, Pont l'Évêque cheese and, finally, Îles Flottantes for dessert. The tantalising vision of a life spent with someone who could cook like that was almost too hard to bear.

From the NowhAirBnB's extensive wine list, Athena Shimmings, who made most of the decisions in their ménage à deux, had chosen a very acceptable Châteauneuf du Pape. Short Head, who usually drank most of the bottle, had experimented that day with filling his mother's glass more frequently than his own.

And the experiment had had an effect. After she had once again expressed the opinion that they'd had a very nice meal and he had confirmed that that was indeed the case, a long silence ensued. Short Head let it ride for a few moments, then glanced across to see what had caused this interruption to the flow.

He could hardly believe his luck. Athena Shimmings was asleep.

And, to compound his good fortune, it was at that moment that Mignon entered to clear the dishes.

It seemed entirely natural for Short Head Shimmings to rise from his chair and envelop her in his arms. Nor, apparently, did his action seem unnatural to her. Though he had to bend down to wrap himself around her pleasingly plump body, they seemed to fit together very well. Before their lips met, he did give an admonitory nod towards his mother, suggesting that, whatever they did, they should keep it quiet.

What they did do was what any two normal people who had been fancying each other rotten for days would have done in the circumstances. A lot of exploration of each other's mouths ensued. And very pleasant it was, too.

Eventually, they broke the mutual suction.

'Oh, Mignon,' said Short Head.

'Oh, Short Head,' said Mignon.

'I have wanted to do that for so long,' said Short Head.

'So have I,' said Mignon.

A literalist might have pointed out that, in this instance, 'so long' wasn't very long at all, since they had only met a few days before. But when did people in love ever have any interest in the opinions of literalists?

'Oh, Mignon,' said Short Head desperately. 'I wish I could get out of this place.'

'I wish you could too.'

'Is there any way you could help me to get out?' he asked.

'I could try,' she said tentatively.

'It would be wonderful if you could,' he said in an anguished voice.

'I'll do my best,' she said.

'Oh, Mignon,' he said, 'you are wonderful!'

More mutual suction ensued. In Mignon's mind was euphoria at the knowledge that Short Head Shimmings wanted to escape his protective environment simply to be alone with her.

In the mind of Short Head Shimmings, who was by no means unromantic, there was a bit of that thought too. But a larger proportion of his brain space was taken up by something else.

Long habit meant that he effortlessly could recall the entire horse racing calendar. And he knew there was a meeting at Exeter racecourse that afternoon.

FIFTEEN

By Como Batinga's standards, this was an easy job.
One of the brothers' snoops had secured the information as to who they should target. And, of course, the Batinga Brothers had a few London taxis which they had used for similar operations.

Their source had accessed the HRH Travel personnel records and found that the member of staff who handled the top-secret end of their business was called Corinne. They also produced a photograph of an immaculately groomed girl in a charcoal-grey uniform.

A couple of evenings of surveillance in Berkeley Square revealed Corinne to be a creature of habit. She exited the front door of the HRH Travel offices at five forty-five sharp. She waited there until a taxi with its yellow crest glowing appeared. Given the time of night, she was clearly used to waiting. On her first night under surveillance, she was there for nearly twenty minutes.

How easy it was, on the third evening, for Como Batinga to wait in his taxi, double-parked in Berkeley Square, engine running, to wait until he saw his quarry emerge on to the pavement. He then switched on his yellow 'TAXI' sign and moved the short distance to where she was hailing him.

He had deliberately kept the lighting in the driver's cubicle to a minimum. Corinne showed no interest in who he was, anyway. He didn't listen when she told him her destination.

But, the moment she was safely seated in the back, with her seatbelt on (what a law-abiding young lady!), he locked the doors from the inside and put his foot down on the accelerator.

'Damone Batinga is a devious man,' said Canary Wolfe over the phone to Mrs Pargeter.

'I already got that impression. Did you tell him what it was about?'

'I said it was in connection to someone who owed money to one of the Batinga companies.'

'Did you mention Short Head Shimmings by name?'

'No, I thought that might come better from you. All too easy for him to give me a blanket no. You, with your feminine wiles, might prove a more effective intermediary.'

Mrs Pargeter was ambivalent on the subject of 'feminine wiles'. She knew she ought to object – and would indeed be letting down the feminist sisterhood if she admitted that such things existed. On the other hand, she knew that they worked. And she knew she had them in spades.

So, the only comment she made was: 'Well, I'll do my best. But is Damone Batinga willing to meet me?'

'Oh yes. He is more than willing to meet you.'

'Excellent. Where? When?'

'Ah. I am afraid it has to be on his terms.'

'Nothing against that.' Mrs Pargeter was pleased she was at home on her own in Lionel's Den. Had Truffler Mason, Hedgeclipper Clinton or Gary been there, they'd already be raising objections about the safety of what she was undertaking.

'So, what are his terms?' she asked.

'Mrs Pargeter, when I met your colleagues, Mr Mason and Mr Clinton, I mentioned to them that Damone Batinga is a member of the same livery company as I am.'

'They told me, yes.'

'Good. Did they also mention that I am currently the master of the company?'

'No, they didn't.' She knew nothing about the livery companies of the City of London but the pride in his voice told her it was appropriate to say, 'Congratulations!'

'Thank you.' Then he rather called out her ignorance by asking, 'Do you know much about the livery companies?'

She owned up straight away that she didn't.

'Well, many of them go back to medieval times. They are, kind of, trade bodies for members of certain professions.'

'And what do they do?'

Canary Wolfe was a little fazed by the question. He was so impressed by his own position as master that it was not a question he'd ever asked himself. 'Well, they have dinners and join together for mutual . . .'

'Backscratching?' Mrs Pargeter suggested.

'There are certain rituals. And we are very deeply involved in charity work.'

'I'm sure you are. And what – so all your members belong to the same profession?'

'That was the basic idea, yes. But the membership of the livery companies does tend to be a bit broader these days. Some of the original trades have gone out of fashion. I mean, I don't think members of The Worshipful Company of Wax Chandlers actually make many wax candles these days. Nor, come to that, do members of The Worshipful Company of Tallow Chandlers make many tallow candles. Both were rather buggered up by advent of electric lighting.

'And so it is with the company of which I am the master. Being of such recent establishment, we deliberately made the qualifications for membership broad. As well as people from the traditional trades of philanthropic moneylending' – that sounded like an oxymoron to Mrs Pargeter – 'we also include people who deal with illegal moneylending.'

'What, you mean loan sharks?'

'No, no, Mrs Pargeter!' He was deeply offended by the suggestion. 'I refer to those who work hard to eliminate the scourge of loan sharks . . . and any other form of illegal moneylending.'

'Who are they then?'

'I refer to the police.'

'Blimey,' said Mrs Pargeter who, when taken by surprise, was prone to using such expressions. 'So, are you saying the coppers come to your dinners?'

'They certainly do. Some of our members hold very high positions in the Metropolitan Police Service.'

'What – so they, kind of, lend respectability to your livery company?'

She had offended him now. Frostily Canary Wolfe replied, 'I can assure you, Mrs Pargeter, that my livery company does not need to be *lent* respectability by anyone. We already have our own innate respectability.'

Mrs Pargeter apologised profusely for an aspersion she might inadvertently have cast on such a fine City institution. Interesting, though, she thought, that the police might rub shoulders at livery company functions with members like Canary Wolfe and Damone Batinga, who might at one time be thought to have had opposing priorities to theirs.

She then compensated for her gaffe with a bit of ego-massage. 'And you say you are master of this livery company? That's an enormously prestigious appointment, isn't it?'

Mollified, Canary Wolfe agreed that it was. 'The trouble is, though,' he went on, 'that my term of office is about to end.' He didn't sound happy about that state of affairs. 'Being master for only a year is very unsatisfactory. You're just beginning to have got through all the complications of the job, you're ready to start making some changes for the good . . . and suddenly, following regulations dreamed up by some nitpicker, you're out on your ear.'

Uncertain whether to respond with more congratulations or with commiserations, Mrs Pargeter said nothing.

Biting back his annoyance, Canary Wolfe said, 'The handover to the new master will take place at a dinner in a couple of days' time.'

'Oh? Right.'

'And the person who will be taking over from me as master is none other than Damone Batinga.'

'Really?' Despite herself, Mrs Pargeter was impressed. For Canary Wolfe to become master of a City livery company was quite an achievement, but accountants have always straddled the line between the legal and the illegal. For the same honour to go to Damone Batinga, whose criminal history was far more extensive and violent . . . well, that was the ultimate whitewash.

'I tell you this,' Canary went on, 'because it is not unrelated to your request for clemency from him.'

'Oh yes?'

'Damone Batinga would be delighted to meet you – and, he implied, to look favourably on your application . . .'

'Yes?'

'If you will agree to be his guest at the imminent livery dinner.'

'Well, that sounds all right,' said Mrs Pargeter. 'Oh, I suppose I should ask . . . which livery company is it you both belong to?'

'It is,' Canary Wolfe, the current master, replied with considerable grandeur, 'The Worshipful Company of Cozeners and Usurers.'

It was strange that The Worshipful Company of Cozeners and Usurers had not come into existence earlier, given the fact that they represented two of the oldest professions in the City of London. But perhaps in previous generations, though there were plenty whose skills would make them suitable for membership, there were few who aspired to such a level of respectability. Most eligible operators, in fact, rather than advertising themselves, preferred to keep firmly out of the limelight.

But events in the world of money, particularly concerning Enron and the implosion of Lehman Brothers, brought the realisation of how narrow the line had become between financial probity and malpractice. And so was established The Worshipful Company of Cozeners and Usurers. Though some of the livery companies could trace their origins back to the 1300s, developments in technology had prompted the establishment in the last century of such novelties as The Worshipful Company of Information Technologists and The Worshipful Company of Management Consultants. So, the cozeners and usurers were in good company.

Most of the City livery companies had two things in common. One, enormous amounts of money from undisclosed sources. And, two, magnificently historic halls in the City of London, wherein all of their mutual backslapping and backscratching could take place.

Now, obviously, the newly-formed The Worshipful Company

of Cozeners and Usurers didn't have a magnificently historic hall in the City of London. But they did have – probably more so than the other Worshipful Companies – enormous amounts of money from undisclosed (very carefully undisclosed) sources.

And they had soon discovered that one of the lesser livery companies, The Worshipful Company of Eel-trap and Coracle Makers, was in dire financial straits. Their main problem was lack of members, due to the vanishingly small number of professionals working in either profession.

So, they were susceptible to a rather mean offer of payment (accompanied by only a minimal amount of physical threatening), which would transfer ownership of their splendid medieval Eel-trappers' Hall to The Worshipful Company of Cozeners and Usurers.

And it was to that venue that Mrs Pargeter had been invited for the livery dinner.

Como Batinga was disappointed. The girl Corinne had put up hardly any resistance at all. She had screamed a bit on the way to the lock-up off New King's Road which he had chosen as the location for her interrogation.

But, when they got there, after he'd locked the gates and joined her in the back of the cab, she had been all submission. He had hardly even got the wire-cutters out of his pocket before she was telling him everything she knew.

That included mention of the Parish Church of St Perpetua the Martyr in Devon. She had no further information as to how the NowhAirBnB hideaway could be accessed, but the address was enough for Como to make a start on this mission of finding Short Head Shimmings.

The trouble was, from his point of view, that since Corinne had given him so much information, he couldn't really find any justification for hurting her. And, even though he was a psychopath, he was a psychopath with standards. He enjoyed causing pain to extract data from recalcitrant witnesses, but having a subject cave in so readily took away the fun.

He wasn't to know, but in behaving the way she did, Corinne was following a precept of the late Mr Pargeter, filtered through the avuncular advice of Hamish Ramon Henriquez. The esteemed strategic mastermind had always said, 'There is no point in people being injured unnecessarily. Submit, blab, give away secrets, in the certain knowledge that, at the appropriate time, other members of my organisation will come and deal with whoever's putting the frighteners on you.'

Also, it has to be said, Corinne was lucky. Como Batinga had slept well the night before. If he hadn't had his full eight hours, he might have been more inclined to inflict senseless violence on her.

As it turned out, though, so deflated was Como Batinga by his victim's readiness to supply the information he required, that he meekly drove the girl back to her home.

And didn't charge her for the fare.

Which meant Corinne was in rather a good mood when she rang HRH to tell him everything that had happened.

Mrs Pargeter had been criticised before, particularly by Truffler Mason, for going out on limbs and acting on her own initiative. So, in her dealings with the private investigator, she followed the old Jesuit principle of telling the truth but not necessarily the whole truth. She reported back to him on her phone conversation with Canary Wolfe. There might, she told Truffler, be a good chance of setting up a meeting with Damone Batinga, under the pretence that it was to reach an accommodation about Short Head Shimmings's gambling debts.

She didn't tell Truffler that the meeting had already been set up.

Nor did she mention Damone's stipulation that he would only play ball if she attended the livery dinner of The Worshipful Company of Cozeners and Usurers as his guest. She was – quite justifiably – fearful that Truffler Mason would immediately stick his oar in and start making elaborate precautions for her safety. She felt confident that she would be under no threat in a public space like the Eel-trappers' Hall.

She also felt confident that she could encourage Damone Batinga's inclination towards mercy for Short Head Shimmings by the deployment of her much-derided feminine wiles.

She had, after all, something of a track record in dealing with gangsters, going right back to the early days of her marriage, when she had faced off the notorious Smith Brothers. The Batingas, she felt assured, couldn't be as bad as them.

So, she didn't want any protective activities by Truffler Mason to put at risk her meeting with Damone Batinga at The Worshipful Company of Cozeners and Usurers' Dinner. She had other plans for things that might happen at that dinner.

To further these plans, she paid another visit to Erin Jarvis, again without letting Truffler know what she was doing.

The young archivist had inherited from her father, Jukebox, an instinctive loyalty to Mrs Pargeter. Whatever information the widow asked for, it would be provided. And if Mrs Pargeter said that her search for such information should be kept a secret from Truffler Mason and Hedgeclipper Clinton, then there was no question that her instructions should be followed.

Mrs Pargeter had arrived at Erin's by cab. Gary was another person who had to be kept out of the loop about what she was doing. Once she had been supplied with coffee, Mrs Pargeter began. 'When I came to see you with Truffler and Hedgeclipper, you suggested that there was a lot more information out there about the Batinga Brothers, if we required it.'

'Acres of the stuff,' Erin agreed.

'All criminal activity?'

'Technically, yes.'

'What does that "technically" mean?'

'It means that: yes, their activities were criminal – and probably still are. But: no, they could never be brought to court for them.'

'"Expensive lawyers" were mentioned before.'

'Yes, Mrs Pargeter, that's certainly part of it. But it's also lack of witnesses who might testify against them.'

'Because of the Batinga Brothers' reputation for violence?'

'Exactly that. They've got the whole thing very neatly sewn up. The majority of witnesses who might have evidence that could bring the Batingas down are – or at least were back then – also members of the criminal fraternity. So, there's very little chance they could say anything that wouldn't also incriminate themselves.'

'Couldn't they . . . what's the expression? "Turn King's evidence"?'

'They *could* . . .' Erin said dubiously. 'But if they did . . . such is the Batingas' reputation for tracking down and dealing with people who've betrayed them, they wouldn't have a restful moment till their lives ended. And there'd be a very strong chance of their lives ending rather prematurely.'

'I get it. But surely there must have been witnesses of the brothers' crimes who had nothing to do with the criminal community?'

'I'm sure there were. But the likelihood of one of them stepping forward to challenge the Batinga Brothers . . .' The grimace on Erin's face filled out the rest of the sentence.

'Well, if you do find someone . . .'

'I'll let you know, Mrs Pargeter. Of course.'

'All we need is one witness to a criminal act committed by the Batinga Brothers, a person whose own reputation is untainted by any connection with the underworld . . .'

'Yes,' Erin agreed. 'And this paragon of virtue must be so brave, so careless of his or her own life, that they'd be prepared to stand up in court and deliver that testimony.'

'You're on the money there!' Mrs Pargeter grinned. 'I'm sure you can unearth someone, Erin.'

'I'm more worried about that person being *unearthed* after the trial,' said a sceptical Erin. 'From a shallow grave.'

SIXTEEN

'You don't think, do you,' asked Holy Smirke, settling in an armchair after another lunch of the divine cassoulet, 'that there's anything going on between our guest and your daughter?'

'Mignon?' Ernestine spluttered. 'Anything going on? You mean anything of a passionate nature?'

'That's rather what I was thinking of, yes.'

'Pah!' said Ernestine, in the way that only a Frenchwoman can say 'Pah!'. 'It is very unlikely. Mignon is a woman in whom the passionate gene is extinct. Indeed, so far as I have observed, in her it never existed. She lacks the essential spark which creates a femme fatale. Which creates, in fact, a Frenchwoman.'

'I wonder, though . . .' said Holy.

'And the idea of her with that Short Fat Shimmings . . .'

'Short *Head* Shimmings.'

'Same difference. But the idea of the two of them together . . . no, it is too ridicule.'

'I wonder . . .'

'No, Holy. Short Arse Shimmings is too—'

'Short *Head* Shimmings.'

'Whatever. He is too much of an Englishman to get involved in anything passionate. Still a mummy's boy. He was not born infused with the passion that inhabits all Frenchmen. He is a typical English cold fish, tied to his mother's apron strings. You could have gone that way too, Holy. Merci Bon Dieu I saved you from that fate. In you I have managed to warm up the famous British sang froid.'

'Yes. Yes, you have,' said Holy Smirke. And, in retrospect, he had been very grateful for Ernestine's intervention in his life.

Mignon was out shopping, so they couldn't at that moment assess whether she was in the grips of a wild and uncharacteristic passion, but Holy and Ernestine, as they did from time to time, went down to check on the other participant in the vicar's imagined romance.

Short Head Shimmings looked as unlike as it was possible to look to a man in the grips of an overwhelming passion. He was transfixed in his chair, staring out of the picture window, and listening to his mother telling him what a nice view they had.

It was apparently not the first time she had voiced this observation. And every iteration of it seemed to have left its mark on the grey face of Short Head Shimmings. A man so reduced, both Holy and Ernestine agreed, was incapable of passion.

The Batinga Brothers had enormous resources of manpower to draw upon when needed. But since most of the individuals involved had criminal records, they were employed only when absolutely necessary. Neither Damone nor Como Batinga, with their proud history of never having been found guilty of any crime, wanted to put that record at risk by associating with known criminals.

This did not mean that respectability for the brothers had brought about a cessation of violence to provide leverage in their transactions. But increasingly they farmed out the actual administration of that violence. New gangs were constantly arriving in London from places like Albania and Romania. They were quite ready, at a price, to accept commissions to hurt people, and to take advantage of the dread that the name of the Batinga Brothers still inspired in their adversaries.

This was a development in their business practices welcomed by Damone Batinga, as he rose up the City hierarchy. It was less appealing to Como, who had always enjoyed getting down and dirty in the course of their missions. For him, organising violence to be enacted by others was a very inadequate substitute for the real thing.

He hadn't mentioned what he was planning to his brother. Damone was getting increasingly pussyfooted about Como having any on-site involvement in their activities. Anyway, the older Batinga was preoccupied at the time by some City dinner that was happening. Como didn't share his interest in The

Worshipful Company of Cozeners and Usurers. Poncing about in dinner jackets repeating meaningless rituals wasn't his idea of fun. For him, nothing compared to hurting people.

So, Como Batinga was very pleased to be driving down to Devon on his own, somewhat belatedly, to sort out the unfinished business with Short Head Shimmings.

Erin Jarvis had access to all kinds of records, ranging from the old ones that she'd digitised from her father's dusty file cards, to resources on the Dark Web that had to be updated virtually on a daily basis. And she'd found a much more efficient way of accessing police records than Jukebox Jarvis had ever discovered.

She was determined to produce results for Mrs Pargeter. She had inherited loyalty to her father's late employer and, the more contact she had with his widow, the stronger that loyalty became.

But it was proving an uphill task, finding evidence of criminal behaviour that could lead to the Batinga Brothers' arrest. They had covered their tracks very well. And all potential witnesses shared a level of complicity in the crimes which ensured they would never testify.

Erin continued her increasingly dispiriting trawl through police records. All she needed was one witness, one innocent witness who had no underworld connections and the Batinga Brothers' empire could be brought crashing down.

But the search for such a paragon was proving slow and unrewarding.

Como Batinga made his approach to the Parish Church of St Perpetua the Martyr slowly and carefully. He parked his car at some distance, so that his arrival could not be observed from the vicarage. Though Corinne had not been able to reveal how to access the NowhAirBnB hideaway itself, she had told him that the on-site minder was the local vicar.

For this mission, Como was armed with more than his signature wire-cutters. They were there, of course, but in another pocket he carried his favourite snub-nosed automatic pistol. He was prepared to use it. He was prepared for there to be collateral damage to people other than his designated quarry. If someone else got hurt, someone else got hurt. That was the way things worked in Como Batinga's world.

The gun felt unfamiliar in his hand. Damone's insistence on making the Batinga Brothers' operations look respectable had narrowed down the opportunities for his brother to go around armed. Part of Como wished that he'd had the opportunity to practise on a rifle range to refurbish his skills. But he wasn't really worried. Muscle memory would come to his aid. And, for him, shooting people was instinctive.

It was early evening, already dark, as Como sidled round the vicarage. Light spilled from the kitchen windows. He peered through, to see Ernestine, whom he had never met, busy with white wine and double cream, whipping up another delight for one very lucky vicar. That evening's treat was to be Fricassée de Lapin à la Crème.

The other windows had their curtains drawn. Como Batinga decided his best approach was going to be the traditional one. He moved to the vicarage's front door.

There was no light overhead when he knocked, but one was switched on from inside before the door was opened, to reveal an attractively rounded woman in her fifties.

'Good evening,' she said.

No time for finesse. Como Batinga drew his pistol. Mignon's eyes widened as he said, 'I've come to get Short Head Shimmings.'

'Gary, can you keep a secret?'

''Course I can, Mrs P.'

'Something just between the two of us?'

'You betcha.' The driver couldn't believe his good fortune. A personal phone call from Mrs Pargeter. And her wanting him to keep a secret 'just between the two of us'.

'I wonder if you'd be free to drive me somewhere this evening?'

''Course I would be.' He had in fact got a first date set up with a rather exciting lingerie model but, when Mrs Pargeter called for his services . . . well, there was no contest. He'd text to put off the girl. 'Where's it to, Mrs P?'

'Place in the City, called Eel-trappers' Hall.'

'Know it well. You in Chigwell?'

'Yes, I am.'

'What time you got to be there?'

'Six thirty for seven.'

'OK. Given the traffic that time of night. I better pick you up quarter to five.'

'Fine. I'll be ready.'

'Look forward to seeing you.' She would never know how heartfelt his words were.

'Oh, and, Gary . . .'

'Yes, Mrs P?'

'It's a bit of a lumber, but could you drive me back after the event?'

''Course I could.'

'I've been told the thing should finish round half past ten.' That was one of the details in the extensive list of instructions about the livery dinner that Damone Batinga had had couriered to her. 'I'm sorry if that means you've got to hang around the City all evening . . .'

'No worries, Mrs P. I got places I can go.'

'And if I need you to fetch me before ten thirty, I'll text you.'

'Fine.'

'I might need to make a quick getaway.'

'"Getaway"?' Gary couldn't believe his luck. He'd be able to demonstrate all of his long-unused skills to her. 'You mean you're looking for a "getaway driver"?'

'What? No, of course I'm not, Gary. I'm not involved in some crime movie.' Though, actually, when she came to think about Damone Batinga's bizarre behaviour, perhaps she was.

Gary covered his disappointment and said, 'I'll be ready the moment you call, Mrs P.'

'Bless you, Gary. I'm so lucky to have you.' More words to feed his dreams. 'See you at quarter to five then.'

Mrs Pargeter put the phone down and opened one of her wardrobes. The livery dinner instructions had been very specific in the matter of dress. In the matter of everything, actually.

It seemed, in a way that the feminist side of her rather resented, that what the female guest wore was dictated by how her male companion was dressed. The guidelines she'd been sent read as follows:

> If Evening Dress is specified on the invitation, you should choose a long dress and have your shoulders covered by sleeves or a stole/scarf.
>
> If Black Tie, a short cocktail dress or evening trousers would be acceptable.
>
> If your host is wearing a lounge suit, then business daywear, a cocktail dress or evening trousers would not be inappropriate.
>
> Use a small evening clutch bag. Avoid a large handbag whether carried or over the shoulder. If you have to bring one, leave it in the secure cloakroom during the dinner itself.

'Well, stuff that for a game of soldiers!' said Mrs Pargeter out loud, as she surveyed the contents of her wardrobe. 'Treating me like I don't know how to dress.'

Though her late husband was not attracted by the arcane rituals of livery companies, she had gone out more while he had been alive. Not lavish, formal occasions, more often intimate dinners à deux in their favoured restaurants. Which did not, after certain events, include Triggers in Theydon Bois. Even if the premises had not been burned to the ground, there was no way Mr Pargeter would patronise anywhere owned by the wretched Lennie, after the way the restaurateur had betrayed him to the Batingas.

So, Mrs Pargeter did not have a wide selection of formal wear to choose from. She could easily have afforded to buy a new ensemble for the Cozeners and Usurers Dinner, but she didn't want to pay Damone Batinga the compliment of going to so much trouble. She had accepted his invitation for a reason, and that reason wasn't to flatter his ego by being submissive.

When she thought about the reason, she felt a pang of

disappointment. It had been her intention to stage a coup at the Eel-trappers' Hall that evening, but she didn't have the right material with which to stage one. She could spend the livery dinner observing Damone Batinga, probing for vulnerabilities, and maybe come away with some useful new insights, but that wasn't what she had hoped the event would provide. She had had higher hopes, but she philosophically reconciled herself to taking a slower course towards the realisation of her ambition. And she turned her attention to the more immediate matter of clothes.

The late Mr Pargeter had always liked her in bright unpatterned colours and her wardrobe contained a spectrum of silk dresses to choose from. He also liked to see her excellent legs, so they were all knee-length. Mrs Pargeter knew she looked equally magnificent in the Burgundy, the Peacock Blue and the Lemon Yellow. It was simply a matter of which one she would go for that evening to dazzle Damone Batinga.

In the course of his ministry – and even more before he was ordained and wore a dog collar only to con little old ladies out of their life savings – Holy Smirke had encountered many men with guns. Faced by the armed and clearly unhinged Como Batinga, he was therefore, like Corinne from HRH Travel, prepared to agree with the late Mr Pargeter's advice that there was no point in people being injured unnecessarily.

He therefore acceded to all of the intruder's requests and, using copious semaphore from his bushy eyebrows, discouraged Ernestine and Mignon from offering any resistance.

Como was by now getting dangerously excited by his proximity to his quarry. Dealing with defaulters on debts to the Batinga Brothers was something he enjoyed possibly more than anything else in his life. And, though Damone was keen on delegating such duties to the gangs from Albania and Romania, this was an issue on which Como stood firm. Damone, the dominant personality, could, in most matters, get his brother to toe the line. But when it was an issue of Como's using his wire-cutters to inflict maximum pain, the older sibling did not even attempt to deter him.

There was no chance of escape for the three hostages. Following the imperative of a man with a gun, Holy, Ernestine and Mignon crossed from the vicarage to the Parish Church of St Perpetua the Martyr. The priest in charge made no protest when ordered to access the NowhAirBnB hideaway.

He yanked the crusader's leg in the approved manner, then led the way down the stairs. Conscious still of the man with a gun behind them, Ernestine and Mignon followed him down.

On the lower level, Holy Smirke keyed in the appropriate code to give access to the inner sanctum.

As she saw them enter, Athena Shimmings observed that the view was even nicer after dark.

Of her son, though, of Short Head Shimmings, there was no trace.

SEVENTEEN

In Lionel's Den in Chigwell, Mrs Pargeter's sartorial pondering was interrupted by the ringing of her mobile. She picked it up. 'Hello?'

The caller was a very excited Erin Jarvis. 'Mrs Pargeter,' she announced, 'I've got it!'

'Got what?'

'The perfect witness we've been looking for!'

'Someone with no criminal connections at all?'

'Absolutely!'

'Tell me more, Erin.'

'It goes back a long way. Over thirty years. I got the information from police records.'

Mrs Pargeter was far too tactful to ask how the archivist could access such secret material.

'It concerns the destruction of a restaurant called Triggers in Theydon Bois.'

'Oh, I know all about that,' said Mrs Pargeter keenly.

'I know you do.'

'Did the police records have lots of detail about my being kidnapped?'

'They didn't mention you by name, but they did say that there was evidence the safe room under the restaurant had been used to hold a kidnap victim.'

'That was me! I was the one who was held down there.'

'You?' Erin couldn't believe how well things were turning out. 'That makes it even easier. You can testify against your abductors.'

'I'd be happy to do that, of course. But there's one thing I don't understand.'

'What's that?'

'I don't understand in what way my kidnapping has anything to do with the Batingas.'

Erin sounded bewildered as she queried, 'Sorry? I'm not with you.'

'I was kidnapped by the Smith Brothers.'

'Ah.'

Erin Jarvis explained. And her explanation explained so much.

'God, I've been so stupid, Erin,' Mrs Pargeter said. 'Lots of things fall into place now. Truffler kept suggesting that I had actually met Damone Batinga and I didn't know what he was talking about. But now I understand. His use of the "Mr Smith" name for security reasons when he booked at Triggers was exactly the same as my husband's! And Lionel never told me the real names of the people who kidnapped me.'

Mrs Pargeter was forced to accept that there were times when her late husband's rule about not discussing his work could lead to confusions.

She was ecstatic. Erin Jarvis had supplied the one detail she had lacked. Or, to put it another way, she, Mrs Pargeter, had supplied Erin Jarvis with the one detail she lacked.

'Anyway,' said Erin, 'I've got all the evidence in a single file. Shall I email it to you?'

'Yes. Then I'll copy it onto a flash drive, so I can produce it when the moment is right.'

'Any idea when the moment might be right?'

'I can't tell you exactly, Erin,' came the reply, 'but, with a bit of luck, very soon.'

Mrs Pargeter made the decision that the Lemon Yellow silk dress would be the one for her to wear to dinner with The Worshipful Company of Cozeners and Usurers.

An event which she was now very much looking forward to.

An event which would see the realisation of all her dreams.

She had known before Erin's revelation that at the Eel-trappers' Hall she'd be the guest of a major crook. Now she knew she would be the guest of a major crook who had organised her kidnapping.

This time, it was certainly personal.

* * *

Como Batinga left all four of the prisoners where they were in the NowhAirBnB hideout. Locking the doors and returning the crusader and his lady from vertical to horizontal had proved simple. Holy Smirke had handed over the relevant codes with lamb-like gentleness.

Mignon had proved equally biddable when he asked her how Short Head Shimmings had managed to get out. Her mother and Holy Smirke were clearly annoyed at what she revealed, but Athena Shimmings seemed untroubled by her son's absence. She had three new people with whom to share her observations about how nice the weather and the view were.

Mignon was less forthcoming about where the escapee might have gone to. She thought he was just getting stir-crazy and was desperate for a change of scene. That was why she'd helped him out. He needed to get some air. For his mental health.

Como Batinga had been unconvinced by this explanation. Short Head Shimmings was probably at greater risk at large than he was in the NowhAirBnB hideaway. He wasn't to know that his pursuer was aware of HRH Travel's operations.

And, as for the mental health suggestion . . . Como certainly didn't buy that. But then, of course, he hadn't spent as long as Short Head Shimmings had listening to his mother Athena talking about nice things. That might have been enough to unhinge anyone.

On the other hand, if his quarry had been let out simply to 'get some air', then there was a strong chance that he would be back fairly soon.

Como Batinga decided to spend his evening in the front room of the vicarage with the curtains drawn back, watching for the returning prodigal. And while he did so, he ate a very good Fricassée de Lapin à la Crème.

What is it with men and their rituals? thought Mrs Pargeter, as she emerged from the Bentley, whose back door Gary, in full peak-capped chauffeur kit, had opened for her. She had told him not to offer her an arm to help her up the stairs of the Eel-trappers' Hall's wonderful medieval frontage.

She was not the only guest arriving on her own, but most

of the women were part of couples. Their expressions, of pained tolerance, did not suggest that their stern-faced dinner-jacketed husbands were much fun to be with. Their money, presumably, cushioned their wives from the pain of attending endless formal functions like livery dinners.

A flunkey inside the door directed Mrs Pargeter to the ladies' coat check. She was wearing a faux-fur wrap, so well made that it looked exactly like real fur. This had on occasion prompted disapproving looks from ecologically conscious women in cloakrooms. Mrs Pargeter enjoyed listening to the comments about her lack of concern for animal welfare, choosing her own moment to reveal her coat's indemnifying label. She had always relished the act of mortifying prigs.

When she removed her coat to hand to the girl behind the counter, there were a few indrawn breaths from the women around her. They didn't arise from the possibility that her fur was real, but from the vivid Lemon Yellowness of what the relinquished coat revealed. Most of the other women had opted for the safety of the Little Black Dress in its rather larger, long-skirted form.

It never occurred to Mrs Pargeter that her choice of costume might be unsuitable. As she billowed back up the stairs, she felt (with justification) that she looked bloody marvellous.

And, relishing her plans for the evening ahead, she felt bloody marvellous, too.

In the anteroom to the Eel-trappers' Great Hall, there was a reception line, for all the world as if someone had just got married. The dignitaries of The Worshipful Company of Cozeners and Usurers stood in fur-lined capes at the end, but the first person an arriving guest would be greeted by was a gentleman in what looked like an academic gown. He carried a staff with some silly gold insignia on the top of it. Canary Wolfe, who had provided some briefing about the evening, had told her that this functionary was known as 'The Beadle'. (She'd never encountered one of those outside *Oliver Twist*.)

Other tips about the evening's protocol which Canary had provided were fairly predictable. To produce a mobile phone at any point was frowned on, and to use one to take photographs, if only of the Eel-trappers' Hall's splendid interior, was an offence which would lead to summary expulsion from the dinner table. There was, however, an official photographer in attendance throughout the evening, and the main speeches would be video recorded.

As to her general demeanour during the evening, Mrs Pargeter was encouraged that, at dinner, she should engage in conversation to the people to her right, to her left and opposite. As to what should be talked about, the advice was that personal relationships, religion and politics were 'not suitable subjects for the dinner table and best avoided'. As a woman guest, she should see that her conversation excluded any subjects that might prove controversial.

Reading between the lines, Mrs Pargeter reckoned she was being told that women should be so grateful for the honour of being included in such a dominantly masculine occasion that they should melt into appropriate obscurity.

Well, Mrs Pargeter had her own views on that instruction.

The role of the beadle at this point of the evening was to ask each arriving guest their name and then bellow it out to the members of the official reception line. As Mrs Pargeter approached, he asked for her name.

'Mrs Pargeter,' she replied.

'Do you have a first name?'

'Mrs Pargeter,' she said. Melita was still a private thing between her and the late Mr Pargeter.

'*Mrs Pargeter!*' the beadle bawled.

She walked along the line of Worshipful dignitaries, shaking any hands that were proffered. The men were all in full white tie evening dress. Their lapels were loaded with badges which made her think of nothing so much as trainspotters.

Canary Wolfe, as Master of The Worshipful Company of Cozeners and Usurers, had told her that he should be addressed as 'Master Cozener', which she duly did when she approached the familiar figure, swamped in a fur-lined cloak that could have been rescued from a Dick Whittington pantomime. His array of badges suggested he'd spotted many more trains than his fellow members had. When Mrs Pargeter asked about them, she was told they were to be referred to as his 'jewels'.

What she wasn't expecting was that, next to the master, was a woman in a Long Black Dress (as opposed to a Little Black Dress). She had the permanently zipped lip of someone who had been to many of these occasions and who 'knew her place'. Mrs Pargeter felt pretty sure she must be Canary's wife but was introduced to her as 'Mistress Cozener'.

And, next, of course, to the retiring master was the master who was about to take his place. Damone Batinga, enrobed in his white tie respectability (and another Dick Whittington robe), looked like monarch of all he surveyed. His expression was one of masterful contempt. For all humanity. But when he surveyed the arrival of Mrs Pargeter, his features were transformed into a huge beam of omnipotence.

For her, it was a strange moment, to see, in a different context, a man whom she had only known previously as her kidnapper. Damone Batinga had aged, certainly. His hair was still dark black, but not without help from a bottle. It was also thinning and inadequately spread over the top of his cranium. And he still had that shield-shaped face of a cartoon hero. She didn't find him any more appealing than she had on their previous encounter in the safe room beneath Triggers Restaurant.

And she wondered how much time could have been saved had she realised that the people she thought of as the Smith Brothers were in fact the Batinga Brothers. But the thought didn't bring any regret. Slight amusement, perhaps. And relish for the revenge she had so punctiliously planned.

'Melita!' cried Damone, clasping her hands in a manner which she found far too proprietorial.

She didn't like the hijacking of her first name either. 'Mrs Pargeter to you,' she said, as if swatting an impertinent child.

But Damone Batinga seemed unfazed by her marked lack of enthusiasm. Swirling her round so that she ended up with an unwelcome arm around her shoulders, he gestured to the photographer to record them as a couple. Mrs Pargeter was just in time to set her face in the mask of someone who is not doing something of their own volition.

She disentangled herself from his clutches and made as if to follow the crowd to where drinks were being served.

'No,' said Damone Batinga. 'You stay here with me.'

'Why?'

'Because you are shortly to become the new Mistress Cozener.'

'What? Look, I agreed to come to this dinner with you as a one-off. There is absolutely nothing permanent going on here.'

'No?' he said. 'How much do you want my brother Como not to hurt Short Head Shimmings?'

Mrs Pargeter stood obediently by the side of the future Master Cozener, to greet the remaining Worshipful Company of Cozeners and Usurers members and guests. To those who expressed surprise at her presence, Damone said jovially, 'Oh, you didn't know? I've had a woman transplant. Meet Melita.'

Quietly, Mrs Pargeter seethed.

At the drinks reception before the dinner, Damone Batinga continued to display her as his trophy, more than ready to introduce her to everyone present.

Amongst those he seemed particularly keen to show her off to was a man who, even though he wore the full white tie ensemble, still looked as if he should have been in police uniform. Damone introduced him as Assistant Commissioner Keith Brodsham of the Met. He reacted when he heard the name of the future master's guest.

'"Pargeter"? That's a name from the past. Name I knew very well in the past.'

'Oh, I get that quite a lot,' said Mrs Pargeter.

'Get what quite a lot?'

'People thinking my surname sounds familiar. There's a character in *The Archers* – you know, the radio series – called Pargeter. That's probably what you're thinking of. I never listen to the programme myself. My own life's far too interesting to bother with soap operas.'

'No. That isn't where I heard the name,' said the assistant commissioner. 'There was a man called Pargeter, with whom I used to have a lot of dealings.'

'Another policeman, was he?' asked an innocent Mrs Pargeter.

'No. This guy was . . . how shall I describe him?'

'I've no idea,' she said, logically enough. 'I don't know who you're talking about.'

'This guy,' Keith Brodsham went on, 'was rumoured to be involved in a lot of crime.'

'Then I certainly wouldn't know who you're talking about,' said Mrs Pargeter primly.

'But we could never get anything to stick on him. Another of those "Teflon Don" characters. I regarded it as a real challenge, trying to get the perisher behind bars. But I never made it. And then I heard the villain died, so I have to put him down as one of my rare failures. Though,' the policeman continued, with a knowing look at Damone Batinga, 'there are others in a similar position who I'm determined to bring down one day.'

The future Master of The Worshipful Company of Cozeners and Usurers chuckled heartily. 'You're never going to get anything on me, Keith. All my businesses are totally above board.' He turned to Mrs Pargeter with a grin. 'This is an old joke between me and Keith, been going on for some years. He keeps suggesting I'm a criminal mastermind and I keep saying, "Where are your witnesses?" Nobody's ever fingered me for a crook.'

'That's because any of the people who might finger you are too involved in crime themselves to come forward.'

'Good one, Keith!' Damone Batinga was continuing to enjoy their old joke.

'Or,' the assistant commissioner went on, 'the ones who might have come forward have a nasty habit of disappearing off the face of the earth.'

'Funny, that, isn't it?' said Damone. And his roar of laughter showed exactly how funny he thought it was.

Keith Brodsham could not help but join in, though there was a seriousness of tone in what he said next. 'But I'm still after you, Damone. In my world there are no closed cases. I go on and on trying to nab the people I know to be villains.'

The future master managed to turn that into a joke, too. Gesturing around the assembly, he said, 'You're spoilt for choice for people like that round here, aren't you?'

When the hilarity prompted by that sally had subsided, Mrs Pargeter said, 'Going back to what you were saying, Assistant Commissioner, about the deceased criminal. My husband is also deceased, but clearly he had nothing but a name in common with the criminal mastermind you were talking about.'

In the vicarage attached to the Parish Church of St Perpetua the Martyr, Como Batinga was not a happy man. He was very tired. In his armchair, looking out of the front window, he kept nearly dozing off during his vigil. But on each occasion he jolted himself back into wakefulness. He wasn't going to miss the return of the escaped Short Head Shimmings.

Inside his head, things were dark. As a long-term sadistic psychopath, he was used to most of his thoughts being sadistically psychopathic. But in that Devon vicarage, as sleepless hour followed sleepless hour, he could sense his thoughts becoming more sadistically psychopathic than usual.

EIGHTEEN

'So,' said Mrs Pargeter, after a long exposition from Damone Batinga about the functions of The Worshipful Company of Cozeners and Usurers, 'it's a bit like the Rotary Club, is it?'

Her host was deeply affronted. 'No, it is nothing like the Rotary Club!'

Looks of shocked disapproval visited the faces of those members and guests who had overheard the exchange.

'Are you saying,' Mrs Pargeter asked, all innocence, 'that The Worshipful Company of Cozeners and Usurers isn't an organisation for men who want to get away from their wives, drink and scratch each other's backs under the guise of charity?'

'It certainly is not,' said the future master. 'And what you have just said, had it come from anyone else, would lead to your immediate ejection from the dinner. However, in your case . . .'

'In my case, what?'

'I will excuse the lapse and hope, as we spend more time together, you will learn a more apposite sense of values.'

Mrs Pargeter was about to snap back that she had no intentions of their spending 'more time together' when she reminded herself of why she was actually at the livery dinner. She was there, partly, to save the serial defaulter on loans, Short Head Shimmings, from the vengeance of the Batinga Brothers. And then to set in motion the decline and fall of their criminal empire.

It might be more sensible for her to keep on the right side of her repellent host until both of those operations were done and dusted.

'So,' meekly, she said, 'I'm sorry, Damone. I spoke out of turn . . .' Something she never thought she'd done in her lifetime. 'It's nerves, I'm afraid. I'm just so overawed by being in such distinguished company in such an amazing venue.'

At least, what she said about the Eel-trappers' Great Hall was true. The huge space had a high vaulted ceiling of ancient timbers, from which a series of fading historic banners hung. The panelled walls were decorated by coats of arms granted to various trade bodies and portraits of former masters of The Worshipful Company of Eel-trap and Coracle Makers, going back to the Middle Ages. (There had been discussions about removing the pictures when The Worshipful Company of Cozeners and Usurers took over the premises. But it was decided, since nobody had a clue who any of them were, anyway, they might as well stay.)

Despite her submissive response to Damone Batinga, Mrs Pargeter was getting pretty sick of the occasion. There had been so much processing and bowing, before they actually got anywhere near eating. The Top Table diners had entered in procession to some pompous music she didn't recognise (in fact, it was the 'Slow March' from Handel's *Scipio*, the regimental march of the Grenadier Guards).

There followed, when they were standing in front of their seats, an incomprehensible – and lengthy – Latin grace, then endless pre-prandial toasts to people who held arcane titles which had no meaning outside the organisation. Mrs Pargeter had once had the misfortune to be a guest at a Masonic Ladies' Night but, when it came to ritual, she realised The Worshipful Company of Cozeners and Usurers made the Masons look quite progressive.

It might seem remarkable that an organisation which had not yet been running a full year had managed to assemble such a raft of traditional rituals so quickly, but the explanation was simple. Many of the members of The Worshipful Company of Cozeners and Usurers already belonged to other livery companies and contributed bits of ceremonial they had witnessed there. It doesn't take long for men obsessed by procedure – and people who want to join livery companies, by definition, fit into that category – to create their own litany of mumbo-jumbo.

Mrs Pargeter found that the food, though, wasn't bad – a few steps up from Rubber Chicken – and the wines were excellent. But, because of the ceremonial element, everything took such an interminably long time.

Mrs Pargeter focused on one of the reasons for her presence at the dinner. 'Damone,' she said, 'I'd really like to talk about Short Head Shimmings.'

'Melita . . .' She winced at his use of the name. 'We don't want to spoil a splendid evening by talking about petty crooks.'

'I don't regard it as spoiling the evening. It's one of the reasons why I'm here.'

'Oh, surely, Melita' – another wince – 'you're here because I asked you to be my guest. To share with me the moment of triumph when I am made Master of The Worshipful Company of Cozeners and Usurers?'

'Yes, that's obviously part of it,' she lied judiciously, 'but I'm also here because I want you and your brother to take the heat off Short Head Shimmings. Incidentally, you have told Como to back off, haven't you?'

'Of course,' Damone Batinga replied smoothly. He didn't think it appropriate to mention the conversation he'd had with his brother earlier in the evening, when he'd urged his brother to 'deal with Short Head Shimmings *once and for all*!'

Mrs Pargeter wanted to continue the conversation, but there was yet another formal event to interrupt it. This was the ceremony of the Loving Cup.

Damone Batinga informed her that The Worshipful Company of Cozeners and Usurers was unusual among livery companies in drinking from the Loving Cup halfway through the dinner, at the end of the main course. Most did it later in the proceedings. He said it was important that guests lift the cup lid with their right hands and raise it aloft. This indicated that their dagger hand was occupied and there was no immediate danger of their stabbing anyone.

He told her that the custom went back to 979 when the Saxon King Edward the Martyr, aged only about sixteen, was assassinated while drinking at a banquet. This seemed to Mrs Pargeter a strange event to celebrate, though, looking round at the assembled members, she could see quite a few potential assassins.

Canary Wolfe, as retiring master, was the first to drink from the Loving Cup. According to protocol, he raised the lid with his right hand, lifted the cup and announced, 'The master drinks to you in a Loving Cup, and bids you all a hearty welcome!'

He then drank and passed the cup to the guest on his right. And so, the game of Pass-the-Parcel continued. Though there were other Loving Cups on other tables, with two hundred diners in the Great Hall, the procedure took a long while.

When it was finally over and the desserts started to appear, Mrs Pargeter hissed at her host, 'All right. Now tell me what you are going to do about Short Head Shimmings.'

Damone said, infuriatingly, 'I have not yet fully decided. But, by the same token, if you do not disagree or take issue with anything I say till the end of the dinner, I might see myself in a position to accede to your request for clemency.'

And, for the time being, Mrs Pargeter had to be content with that. But she wasn't too worried. She did have other plans for how the evening might pan out.

She had a long time to wait before her moment arrived. The collection by the waiting staff of empty coffee cups by no means signified the end of the evening. The distribution of port, with its complicated rules for passing the bottle, led to the Loyal Toast, no longer the signal for the smokers to start smoking. Before the toast, the first verse of the National Anthem was sung.

And the Loyal Toast was not the only one. Others were all announced by the beadle, with frequent use of his gavel, which he clearly enjoyed wielding. The second was the Civic Toast to 'The Lord Mayor, the Sheriffs and City of London Corporation'.

Countless other toasts followed, announced by someone called the Senior Warden. In her mind Mrs Pargeter considered comparing the proceedings to watching paint dry, but realised the comparison didn't work. Paint does eventually dry, but there was no indication that the proceedings of The Worshipful Company of Cozeners and Usurers' Livery Dinner would ever end.

Then, with further toasting, the first guest speaker was

announced. 'First?' thought Mrs Pargeter with an almost audible groan. How many were there going to be?

The first speaker was duller than a Christmas round-robin letter. He talked about the City, its former prosperity, its current diminished prosperity and its prospects for that prosperity to diminish further in the future. He sat down to a storm of applause. Maybe, Mrs Pargeter thought, the reaction was down to all those letters after his name.

Then, with more gavelling and toasting from the beadle, the second guest speaker was introduced. He was the evening's designated Light Relief. He had clearly been doing the same routine for decades, usually to all-male audiences. His concession to changed sensibilities in the current era was to keep saying, 'I probably shouldn't tell this joke with ladies present . . .' before adding, 'but ladies these days, equal in everything, are at least as broadminded as men are.' And then proceeding to tell the joke, anyway.

The men present roared at his 'cheeky chappie' audacity, and the women made sure they laughed at exaggerated volume, to show what good sports they were.

To Mrs Pargeter's mind, it was all just schoolboy smut. When, oh, when would they get to the ceremonial handover of office from the current master to the new one?

Even Arctic winters end, and finally the moment arrived, bolstered by yet more meaningless ritual. Canary Wolfe went on at length about how much he had enjoyed his year in office, the significant changes he had made during his year in office, in how good a condition he felt he was leaving The Worshipful Company of Cozeners and Usurers after his year in office and how pleased, at the end of his year in office, he was to be handing over to such a highly suitable candidate to take over the mastership.

He could not infuse that last sentiment with much enthusiasm. If Mrs Pargeter hadn't heard him saying it himself, she would have intuited from his tone that he thought a year was far too short a term in which to make a proper impression. And that the man he was handing over to was not nearly as suitable for high office as he had been.

During the applause for Canary's speech, Damone whispered fiercely to Mrs Pargeter. 'Remember – don't question anything I say. You put a foot wrong, and I will unleash the full destructive power of my brother Como on your unfortunate mate Short Head Shimmings. Got that?'

While she digested the threat, with much more toasting and insincere praise for his predecessor, Damone Batinga then addressed his audience, many of whom were by now comatose from the evening's drinking. The younger women were looking at their watches and worrying about babysitters.

The new Master of The Worshipful Company of Cozeners and Usurers rose to the microphone and began his speech with a run-of-the-mill and clearly insincere encomium on his predecessor. He then said his intention, as their master, was to tread firmly in the footsteps so carefully laid down by Past-Master Neville Wolfe. That promise sounded equally insincere. He would clearly use his new-found status in whatever way he felt fit.

Damone Batinga then went on to say, 'Tonight is a time of double celebration for me. Not only have I achieved my lifelong ambition of becoming master of one of the City of London's esteemed livery companies, I have achieved something equally important at what can only, by the same token, be described as the personal level.

'Some of you may have noticed that this evening, at my side, there is sitting a lady, whom you have possibly not seen before. Not that, of course, you will now be able to forget her, given her rather distinctive choice of dress.'

There was a bit of uneasy laughter. Mrs Pargeter wasn't the only one present who wondered where he was going with this.

'Well, I'm pleased to announce that, not only is Melita my guest for tonight's dinner –' he flashed a warning look at her, as if to say, If you argue with anything I say, it's curtains for Short Head Shimmings – 'but also, that the two of us are going to get married!'

That woke up even the most comatose of the diners. Applause ensued. The official photographer was instantly on the scene, snapping away at the happy couple.

Damone Batinga went on. 'I have held a candle for this lady for many years. She was married to someone in the same business as myself. He was someone I used to work with.'

'Work *against*, don't you mean?' shouted an unidentified voice somewhere in the Great Hall.

Damone ignored the interruption and went on. 'So, today, members and guests of The Worshipful Company of Cozeners and Usurers, I feel doubly blessed. By the same token, me and my Lady in Yellow look forward to a very happy future together. Don't we, Melita my love?'

Mrs Pargeter rose to her feet. 'May I tell everyone,' she asked sweetly, 'just how much I look forward to a very happy future together, Damone?'

Her adorer smiled. In the end, everyone came round to his way of thinking. He was pleased that, with Melita, it had happened so quickly.

He wasn't expecting the sharp jab of her elbow, with which she nudged the new master away from the microphone and took hold of it.

'Members and guests,' she announced, 'if Damone thinks I'm going to keep my mouth shut when we're married . . . well, he's got another think coming!'

This prompted quite a big laugh from the assembled throng. It also eased the anxiety in her putative husband's face.

But his reprieve wasn't to last for long, as Mrs Pargeter continued. 'Mind you, in saying "when we are married", I am effectively saying, "when hell freezes over". There is no way I would ever consider marrying a member of the criminal community!'

'Ah, but he's not a *convicted* member of the criminal community,' shouted a voice. Mrs Pargeter had no difficulty in identifying this one. It belonged to an assistant commissioner of the Metropolitan Police.

'Don't worry, Keith,' she cried. 'He will be soon! So far you haven't had a reliable witness who can testify to his criminal activities. Well, you've got one now! It's me!'

'This woman is clearly unwell,' shouted Damone Batinga, trying to regain his position at the microphone. Another pointed elbow put him in his place (in more than one sense of the expression).

Mrs Pargeter went on. 'Some thirty years ago, I was kidnapped by Damone Batinga and his brother, Como. I can provide evidence of that crime, provide evidence that they had a stash of cocaine hidden under a restaurant in Theydon Bois. The restaurant's owner went down for the crime of possession, but it was the Batinga Brothers who were doing the drug-running.

'And, *by the same token* . . .' – how she enjoyed throwing his infuriating verbal tic back at him – 'I can provide evidence of a lot of other crimes!'

She reached into her cleavage and extracted a flash drive from the centre junction of her bra. Then, to the astonishment of the other guests, she climbed over the Top Table into the middle of the room.

Handing the flash drive to Keith Brodsham, she said, 'You'll find evidence to convict them both there. And, when you want to take down my witness statement, I will, of course, be happy to oblige!'

With that, she strode out of the Great Hall. She was aware of some rumblings of discontent among the diners, but she didn't wait to confront them.

What she wasn't to know was that, having heard of one person prepared to testify against the Batinga Brothers, a lot of other people in the room felt emboldened to add their own experiences to the testimony. The one thing the Batingas had never inspired was affection.

Most members of The Worshipful Company of Cozeners and Usurers present that evening would be happy to help bring them down.

Mrs Pargeter reckoned she would leave her faux-fur wrap to be picked up another day.

As she exited the Eel-trappers' Hall, she was unsurprised to find Gary waiting, with the back door of the Bentley held open for her. He always had a good sense of timing.

'Where to, Mrs P?' he asked, once she was safely ensconced.

'First, to pick up Truffler,' Mrs Pargeter replied. 'Then, foot down all the way to Devon.'

Gary couldn't have been happier. Mrs Pargeter in the back of his car – and permission to show off his old getaway driving skills.

NINETEEN

Short Head Shimmings spent an uncomfortable and frustrating night. The euphoria of being out of the NowhAirBnB hideaway soon diluted when he realised he still had no access to either laptop or mobile phone. Mignon, he knew, had, at his mother's request, taken his away for 'safekeeping'. But he hadn't thought to ask her, before she let him out, where she had put them. And there appeared to be no doorbell on the crusader's tomb, which might allow him to summon Mignon back again.

Presumably, she'd hidden the laptop and mobile phone in the vicarage somewhere. But going up to the door, knocking and asking to be let in would simply alert Holy Smirke and Ernestine to the fact of his escape.

And who knew how long Mignon would be stuck in the hideaway, transfixed by Athena Shimmings telling her how nice everything was?

He was also feeling a little guilty about how he'd treated Mignon. To say that he'd rather be released from his prison to place a bet than to spend time alone with her, was, he knew, not a procedure recommended in advice columns about starting new relationships. Though he hadn't met many women except for his mother, some masculine folk memory told him that they were sensitive creatures, easily upset by lack of attention from men who'd expressed interest in them.

But, in a true gambling addict, the urge to have a bet predominates over all other considerations. After the agony of his incarceration and hearing how nice everything was, Short Head was desperate to have a punt on something. Anything. He'd missed that day's meeting at Exeter and couldn't wait till the racing started up again there the following afternoon. But, of course, you didn't have to be on a racecourse to make a bet.

He had noticed, on a map he'd found in the enlarged car

boot in which he and his mother had travelled to Devon, that the Parish Church of St Perpetua the Martyr was situated some seven miles away from the nearest town. Where, he realised, would lie the solution to his problem. He set out to walk there.

He wasn't a regular walker, and the days spent ingesting Mignon's wonderful cuisine hadn't done a lot for his general fitness. The walk was hard work. And his mood was not improved by the fact that, as soon as he started on his trek, it began to rain. Heavily. The wetness had soon penetrated the shoulders of his Teddy Boy jacket and flattened the quiff in his dyed hair.

It was still dark when he reached the town. To rest his blistered feet and sodden body and get some sleep, he deposited himself on the doorstep of his destination.

Back at the vicarage, Como Batinga wasn't having a good night either. He kept making himself cups of coffee to keep awake, but still there was no sign of the prodigal debtor returning to the Parish Church of St Perpetua the Martyr.

As the sleepless hours passed, within the psychopath's twisted mind, homicidal urges grew stronger.

Mrs Pargeter wasn't getting much sleep either, but she was in a much better state of mind than Short Head or Como. After her triumph at The Worshipful Company of Cozeners and Usurers Livery Dinner, she felt positively ecstatic.

The Bentley had duly picked up Truffler Mason, and Gary was now driving at his much-loved getaway speed through the empty nighttime roads towards Devon.

Because Gary's car hire service thought of everything, there was a warm blanket to wrap around Mrs Pargeter's Lemon Yellow silk dress, and a contrastingly cold bottle of champagne in the minifridge. She and Truffler shared this as she brought him up to speed with what had happened during the last twenty-four hours.

He was, needless to say, deeply upset by the fact that she, in spite of his many injunctions about such situations, had taken it upon herself to tackle the livery dinner alone.

'But if I had told you,' she argued plaintively, 'you would have forbidden me to attend, wouldn't you?'

Truffler Mason could not deny that this was true.

'So, I'd never have had the opportunity to confront Damone Batinga about his criminal activities, which I witnessed. And he'd still have an unblemished criminal record.'

'It still is unblemished,' said Truffler mournfully. 'He hasn't been charged and convicted yet. Damone Batinga has often been close to being arrested, but his expensive lawyers have worked their devious magic, and the cops have never managed to nab him yet.'

'A large number of the Metropolitan Police Service were actually present last night. And probably a lot of lawyers. All the police have been lacking is a credible witness with no criminal connections. And now they've got that. Me!'

Truffler did not take issue about her assertion that she had 'no criminal connections'. He had always been happy to believe what she believed.

'You weren't at the dinner long enough to see whether Damone Batinga left unimpeded? Or whether he was actually arrested at the scene?'

'No, but, given that dossier Erin provided on his activities, it's only a matter of time.'

'Maybe. But you do realise, Mrs P, what your public denunciation of the Batinga Brothers has done?'

'It's brought them to justice.'

'It may end up doing that, but what it's done in the short term is to put you into grave jeopardy.'

'How so?'

'As you've just said, the police have now got their credible witness.'

'Yes. Me.'

'But, if that credible witness were eliminated before she got the opportunity to testify, then the Batinga Brothers would once again be untouchable.'

'Ah,' said Mrs Pargeter. 'I hadn't thought of that.'

* * *

Como Batinga might nearly have been dozing off, but he was fully awake when he answered the ringing of his mobile. 'Hello?'

'It's me.'

The brothers' voices were so familiar to each other, they never needed to identify themselves.

'Where the hell are you?' demanded Damone.

'I'm in Devon.'

'Why the hell are you in Devon?' The older brother's habitual short fuse seemed to have been radically shortened.

'I've tracked down Short Head Shimmings. I'm going to deal with him.' Como refrained from saying that his quarry was currently absent.

'Ah. That could be good.' Damone sounded relieved.

'How, good?'

'I think Mrs Pargeter's protecting him.'

'Mrs Pargeter? What, the one we kidnapped way back in—?'

'The very same. I think she's probably, even now, on her way down to Devon to save Short Head Shimmings. But what matters is that, as of last night, Mrs Pargeter has suddenly become our Number One Enemy.'

'How so?'

'Haven't got time for the details now. Just take my word for it, our whole operation will go belly-up if Mrs Pargeter is not eliminated as soon as possible.'

'Leave it to me,' said Como with relish.

'So, look, keep an eye out for the arrival of Mrs Pargeter. She'll probably be accompanied by Truffler Mason. Remember him?'

'And how?'

'And Gary.'

'I remember him, and all. Kid driver, worked for Mr Pargeter, didn't he?'

'That's right. They all used to work for Mr Pargeter. And they're trying to get revenge on us on his behalf. Any others of their gang down in Devon?'

'There's a dodgy vicar and three women. Don't know where they fit in. They seem to be kind of minders for Short Head.'

'Are they on the loose?'

'No, they're all safely locked up.'

'Good. Now, listen, Como. If my instinct's right, Mrs Pargeter and her lot are going to be arriving where you are pretty soon, with a view to rescuing Short Head Shimmings.'

'Yes.' It was time to own up. Fearing the wrath of his brother when he told him, Como admitted, 'Short Head is, currently . . . momentarily . . . missing.'

But the expected storm of recrimination didn't happen. Instead, Damone said, 'Never mind him. We can deal with that crook whenever we need to. More important right now is that you eliminate Mrs Pargeter.'

'Will do,' said the obedient psychopath. 'One thing, Damone, given that Short Head seems to have escaped, where do you think I should look for him?'

'Has he got a laptop with him? Or a mobile phone?'

'I'm pretty sure he hasn't.'

'Well then, if that's the case, there's only one place to look for a gambling addict, isn't there?'

Como didn't know, but his brother supplied him with the obvious answer. 'Anyway,' Damone went on urgently, 'don't worry about Short Head for the moment. The most important thing is for you to kill Mrs Pargeter!'

'And what about the others? The people with her?'

'Kill them all!' said Damone Batinga.

On Truffler Mason's advice, Gary slowed the Bentley down as they approached the Parish Church of St Perpetua the Martyr and its vicarage. 'It's quite possible the Batinga Brothers are staking the place out. I've been trying to contact Holy Smirke and there's no reply, which I would say was ominous.'

'I hope I haven't got him into trouble,' said Mrs Pargeter.

'It's not your fault,' Truffler reassured her, 'that you've come up against a pair of the most vicious gangsters currently operating.'

'No, I suppose that's true,' said Mrs Pargeter.

'Stop, Gary!' said Truffler.

The Bentley's headlights had caught a reflection of metal ahead. Drawing closer, they could see it was a car, close to the front entrance of the Parish Church of St Perpetua the Martyr.

'OK.' Truffler took charge. 'That belongs to someone connected to the Batinga Brothers. Time for us to hide. Gary, get the Bentley into the woods, somewhere where we're hidden from the road.'

The driver obeyed the instruction. Soon, the great vehicle was out of sight, but through a small gap in the foliage, Gary could still see the Batingas' car.

'I'm just going to do a recce,' said Truffler, uncoiling his long body to get out. 'You stay here, Gary. And guard Mrs Pargeter with your life!'

Never had the driver been given a more welcome instruction.

After the phone call from his brother, as well as feeling extremely homicidal, Como Batinga was also conflicted. He now knew that their urgent priority was the elimination of Mrs Pargeter. But, at the same time, he had been building up his expectations about how he would eliminate Short Head Shimmings, and he didn't want to be cheated of that pleasure.

Also, Damone had given him a very heavy clue as to where he'd find his original quarry. The arguments went round and round in his head. Killing Mrs Pargeter was the first priority, yes, but she hadn't arrived at the Parish Church of St Perpetua the Martyr yet. Whereas Short Head Shimmings also needed to be killed at some point, and he was easily accessible.

What really appealed to Como was the idea of killing them all at the same time.

He continued pondering his options. While he did so, he felt a pain in his head building. It was the one that came when he hadn't had enough sleep. It didn't respond to aspirin or paracetamol. The only cure he'd ever found for it was killing someone.

Truffler Mason returned to the Bentley, silently closing its back door and sliding into the seat next to Mrs Pargeter.

'Como Batinga's there,' he said, 'watching from the front window. No other lights on in the vicarage, which maybe isn't surprising this time of night. But I get the feeling he's the only one in the house.'

'What do you reckon he's doing?'

'Obviously, Mrs P, waiting for any activity from the church. Or, possibly even more worrying from our point of view, waiting for reinforcements.'

'All those Albanians and Romanians they use?' suggested Gary.

'Could be,' said Truffler, more doom-laden than ever. 'If they've got superior numbers, then we will have a problem.'

'Then surely,' said Mrs Pargeter, 'there's a strong argument for taking out Como Batinga before the reinforcements arrive.'

'Yes. He's a tricky customer, though.'

'Oh, come on, Truffler,' said Gary. 'There's only one of him and two of us.'

'Three,' asserted Mrs Pargeter.

But the bonus of her participation did not lift Truffler Mason's mood. He continued dolefully, 'Anyway, in the unlikely event of our taking out Como Batinga, if Holy Smirke and the others are down in the hideaway, we can't get them out.'

'Why not?' said Mrs Pargeter. 'We know which leg of the crusader to pull, don't we?'

'Yes, but down the bottom of those stairs there's a keypad and—'

'Are you suggesting,' asked Mrs Pargeter, rather magnificently, 'that I didn't memorise the numbers of the code when we were last here?'

Truffler was cut off in his expressions of admiration by a hiss from Gary. 'There's someone going to the car!'

All three peered through the break in the leaves to see, in the opening light of dawn, Como Batinga get into the car and drive off through the rain.

There was only one in the nearby town, so inevitably that was the one he went to. On the doorstep, fast asleep, was an extremely wet Short Head Shimmings.

Shaken awake, he looked up and recognised the person who had shaken him.

'Como!' he said. 'Just the person I want to see. I know I owe you a bit, but could you see your way to lending another hundred? In cash. You see this betting shop doesn't open till nine, but I've just got that feeling today's going to be my lucky day and—'

He was interrupted by being grabbed and chucked into the boot of a car. Como Batinga had other plans for him, promising a day that might not be so lucky.

Como had not locked the vicarage door, so Truffler just did a quick check that there was no one inside before they crossed to the Parish Church of St Perpetua the Martyr. Gary did the honours of raising the crusader's leg and, at the bottom of the stairs, Mrs Pargeter's memory for keypad numbers proved reliable.

The internees, Holy Smirke, Ernestine and Mignon, were extremely relieved by their arrival. Though they hadn't starved while they were down there, they had worried about being held at the whim of a homicidal psychopath.

Athena Shimmings, on the other hand, said the time they had had together had been 'very nice'.

Mignon was desperate for one piece of news they couldn't provide for her. Where was Short Head?

That question, sadly, was answered rather earlier than they might have wished. Just as they were about to climb out to freedom, the light at the top of the stairs was blocked by two approaching figures. A very wet and frightened-looking Short Head, Elvis quiff flat across his cranium. Followed by Como Batinga, holding his semi-automatic pistol into the small of his prisoner's back.

'Back down again!' said the gunman to the would-be escapees, jabbing at the man in front of him. They all obeyed.

'Oh, how convenient,' said Como. 'Mrs Pargeter. My brother and I have been trying to find you and you've just walked in here of your own accord. Isn't that nice?'

'Very nice,' Athena Shimmings agreed.

Como Batinga pushed Short Head forward, then, with one neat move, redirected the barrel of his pistol from the small of his back to the small of Mrs Pargeter's.

Truffler Mason and Gary both moved forward on the attack,

but they were quickly dissuaded when their opponent said, 'If you think I wouldn't use this gun, then you're talking to the wrong person. I am going to kill Mrs Pargeter. In fact, you may as well know, I'm going to kill all of you. The only thing I have to decide is which order I will do it in.'

The pain in his head was building to an almost unbearable intensity. He longed for the relief that a murder would bring him. He raised his gun-free hand to his forehead as if he could somehow wipe the pain away.

That moment of distraction was all that Gary needed. Without a thought for his own safety, he hurled himself across the room, his bodyweight sending Como Batinga flying. While the two men grappled on the floor, Truffler stamped a heavy foot down on Como's right wrist. He cried out in pain, as the gun flew out of the hand. Truffler picked the weapon up and trained it on the would-be assassin.

'Well, thank you very much,' said Mrs Pargeter. 'He had me worried there for a moment. Very good of you, Truffler.'

'Very nice,' Athena Shimmings agreed.

'So, Como,' said Mrs Pargeter, as the unarmed villain sheepishly stood up, 'it seems like we have the upper hand now, don't we? No longer will you and your brother terrorise decent citizens. The entire Batinga empire is about to fall apart!'

'I wouldn't be so sure of that,' said a new voice.

They turned to see Damone Batinga coming down the stairs, armed with a rather bigger machine pistol than his brother's. He was still wearing his white tie and tails, though they were somewhat grubbier than they had been the night before at the Eel-trappers' Hall. He must have escaped the attentions of Assistant Commissioner Keith Brodsham and driven like a maniac down to Devon.

'Give Como his gun back, Truffler,' he said silkily, the barrel of his own pointing firmly at Mrs Pargeter. 'And the rest of you – all except for Mrs Pargeter – move back, as close to the walls as you can get.'

There was nothing Truffler or the others could do but obey. Taking the proffered weapon, Como stood beside his brother, the pair of them making everyone in the room freeze.

Damone moved slowly towards his target, the gun barrel still trained on her head. 'I'm sorry our relationship has to end like this, Melita.'

In spite of her jeopardy, she winced at the use of her name.

'When I offered you marriage last night, I meant it. But there's a long history of people killing the things they love, and I'm afraid you're just about to become part of that.'

He was by now right beside her, the point of his gun nestling under her ear.

'I'm sorry, you've gone too far. You are, as you said last night, the only witness who can bring down everything that the Batinga Brothers operation has worked so hard to achieve. I'm afraid I can't allow that to happen. So, if you know one, Melita, say a prayer. Because I'm going to kill you on a count of three.'

Mrs Pargeter didn't say a prayer, though she did know a few. She didn't need prayers. She was going to survive. Though how that happy outcome could be achieved . . . was a piece of information she did not currently have.

'One . . .' Damone intoned. 'Two . . .' The silence seemed to stretch forever. 'Three!'

But nothing happened. Damone Batinga seemed to be as frozen as his audience. His trigger finger could not move.

Dashing himself away from Mrs Pargeter, he cried in anguish, 'I cannot do it! I cannot kill the woman I love!'

'Well, I can!' Como Batinga, his brain bursting with pain, leapt forward and pointed his pistol straight at Mrs Pargeter's forehead. The gun slipped. It didn't feel secure in his hand. He hadn't adjusted his habitual grip to take into account a missing little finger. (Good old Hedgeclipper Clinton!)

But the moment of hope didn't last. Como Batinga re-asserted his control of the gun and pressed it against Mrs Pargeter's temple.

What happened next happened so quickly that those present spent a considerable time afterwards discussing the precise sequence of events. What they did all recall, though, was that Damone Batinga leapt forward to divert his brother's gun barrel. Also, Como Batinga's gun had been pointing towards the window when it went off and, in the confusion, Damone's also fired in the same direction.

The huge glass pane shattered, falling down like a heavy and extremely short hailstorm.

Como refocused his pistol on Mrs Pargeter, but Damone grappled his body to stop him firing. The brothers, clasped together, stumbling on the seaward side of the room, struggled to land blows on each other. Then, missing their footing, and still locked in a less than fraternal embrace, they both fell through the absent window, down on to the rocks below.

'Without the window,' said Athena Shimmings, 'the view's even nicer, isn't it, Cecil?'

But from her son she did not get the anticipated response of agreement. He was preoccupied, in the arms of his beloved Mignon, with their lips once again conjoined.

TWENTY

The winding-up of the Batinga Brothers' empire, without either of the two principals involved, was speedy. Erin Jarvis's research, on the flash drive given to him, prompted Assistant Commissioner Keith Brodsham to unleash the full powers of the Met on further investigations. And the outcome of those investigations showed how far-reaching had been the tentacles of the Batinga criminal organisation.

A lot of cold cases got solved, including the mysterious conflagration at Triggers Restaurant in Theydon Bois some thirty years before. And, with the Batinga Brothers themselves gone, many witnesses of their wrongdoing, who had previously kept quiet, fearing for their safety, stepped forward to testify.

In the end, very few of the brothers' former associates spent time in jail. Some made bargains with the police, exchanging information for freedom. Some took their stories of collaboration with the Batingas to their graves.

A few members who had attended The Worshipful Company of Cozeners and Usurers Livery Dinner did get investigated and went to jail for making their Cozening and Usury a little too public. The City of London does, after all, have standards.

The way events turned out proved beneficial to Canary Wolfe. The disgrace – not to mention death – of the new Master of The Worshipful Company of Cozeners and Usurers left an obvious gap. Who better to fill it than the previous incumbent, a man without the smallest stain on his character, who had made such a good job of guiding the first year of the new livery company?

In his second year, he managed to get through the various livery committees a change in the company's regulations. Thenceforward, the master did not have to be replaced each year. If he was doing a good job and nobody objected, he could stay in post as long as he liked. And Canary Wolfe was determined that his tenure would be coterminous with his death. A development which, in her customary tight-lipped way, his wife put up with.

In Devon, the destruction of the hideaway's window had led to a great deal of media coverage. Before and after photographs showing the disguised frontage meant that the premises could no longer be used by HRH Travel as NowhAirBnB secure accommodation. It soon became a regular Airbnb, still with Holy Smirke and Ernestine as the on-site wardens.

The venue's minor notoriety made it very popular, and bookings stretched far into the future. One week a year, though, was reserved for Athena Shimmings, who arrived each time with a new female companion with whom she could share thoughts about how nice the view was. (Remarkably, though asked, none of the female companions were available to come back a second year.)

The need for these female companions arose from the fact that Athena and her son no longer cohabited. Short Head had actually married Mignon. The couple had both escaped dominant and difficult mothers, which is a happy outcome for any romantic story.

The marriage itself was conducted at the Parish Church of St Perpetua the Martyr. Holy Smirke conducted the service. And, since he was feeling particularly bonhomous, at the same time he married the bride's mother.

Now, opinions differ as to whether a vicar can conduct his own wedding ceremony. Well, no, they don't actually differ that much. There is a general consensus, amongst senior members of most religions, that a vicar cannot conduct his own wedding ceremony.

But Holy Smirke had always been one for bending the rules. And, as one of the wedding guests commented to him, 'If there's some doubt over the legitimacy of your marriage, then that gives you a handy let-out . . . should you need it.'

The guest who made that comment clearly knew Holy Smirke's character well. In fact, it was Mrs Pargeter.

Her remark was one that the vicar sometimes, in moments of minor strife, quoted to his wife. But he never did really want a 'handy let-out' from his marriage. There were too many compensations that came with it. Not to mention that cassoulet . . .

Attaining freedom in their fifties was a blissful experience for Short Head and Mignon. They suited each other perfectly and neither regretted meeting at a time of life when children were not an option. All they needed was each other.

And they found a brilliant way of dealing with the one thing that might have cast a shadow over their happiness – Short Head's gambling addiction. The deal was that he could have two bets a day. He could try to guess what Mignon was going to cook him for lunch, and then try to guess what Mignon was going to cook him for supper.

This arrangement worked very well. One result was that Mignon, trying to outfox her husband, experimented with ever more exotic culinary delights. And Short Head soon seemed to stop worrying that his winnings were not paid in money, but in gastronomic and physical pleasures.

Another result was that Short Head Shimmings's waistband, in common with his new father-in-law's (or, because we're talking about Holy Smirke, his father-probably-not-in-law's), expanded considerably.

Another man with a habit to break was less successful. Concrete Jacket could never quite wean himself off the habit of going to prison from time to time. It was never his fault. His latest sentence arose from some bathroom fittings his client had ordered somehow ending up adorning a new estate in Bulgaria.

His fiancée Tammy said she'd never known a man who was so unlucky with the staff he employed. She still adored him, but their wedding had to be put off yet again.

* * *

Mrs Pargeter continued her life of pampering and philanthropy. She still took herself out on her own for self-indulgent meals at local hostelries. When she wanted a more substantial blow-out, she got Gary to drive her up to Greene's Hotel, where Hedgeclipper Clinton ensured there was always a suite ready for her.

There, she would often dine with Truffler Mason, Hamish Ramon Henriquez, Canary Wolfe and other former associates of the late Mr Pargeter.

And, if the conversation ever teetered over the edge into the subject of criminality, she would always say, 'Ooh, I wouldn't know about that.'

Which was, of course, always true.